"Why should I be afraid?" Autumn said defensively.

"More than once you've told me you don't like to be touched—a minute ago, while I was touching your face, you were so nervous I thought you were going to faint...."

As though to demonstrate, Saul reached out and trailed a fingertip down her cheek, making her jump violently.

With a glint of triumph, he asked, "Does everyone's touch affect you so strongly, or is it just mine?"

LEE WILKINSON lives with her husband in a three-hundred-year-old stone cottage in an English village, which most winters gets cut off by snow. They both enjoy traveling and recently, joining forces with their daughter and son-in-law, spent a year going around the world "on a shoestring." Her hobbies are reading and gardening and holding impromptu barbecues for her long-suffering family and friends.

Blind Obsession

LEE WILKINSON

SWEET REVENGE

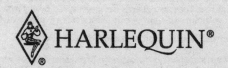

HARLEQUIN®

TORONTO • NEW YORK • LONDON
AMSTERDAM • PARIS • SYDNEY • HAMBURG
STOCKHOLM • ATHENS • TOKYO • MILAN • MADRID
PRAGUE • WARSAW • BUDAPEST • AUCKLAND

ISBN 0-373-80546-2

BLIND OBSESSION

First North American Publication 2000.

Copyright © 1995 by Lee Wilkinson.

All rights reserved. Except for use in any review, the reproduction or utilization of this work in whole or in part in any form by any electronic, mechanical or other means, now known or hereafter invented, including xerography, photocopying and recording, or in any information storage or retrieval system, is forbidden without the written permission of the publisher, Harlequin Enterprises Limited, 225 Duncan Mill Road, Don Mills, Ontario, Canada M3B 3K9.

All characters in this book have no existence outside the imagination of the author and have no relation whatsoever to anyone bearing the same name or names. They are not even distantly inspired by any individual known or unknown to the author, and all incidents are pure invention.

This edition published by arrangement with Harlequin Books S.A.

® and TM are trademarks of the publisher. Trademarks indicated with ® are registered in the United States Patent and Trademark Office, the Canadian Trade Marks Office and in other countries.

Visit us at www.eHarlequin.com

Printed in U.S.A.

CHAPTER ONE

AUTUMN knew she had been an absolute idiot to come. Knew it. Admitted it. She was taking a terrible risk. But she couldn't remember a time when she hadn't loved Saul. It seemed he'd always been a part of her, and the longing, the need to see him just once more, had been too great to resist.

She sat bolt upright on the leather chair, stiff and unnaturally still, as though any sign of fidgeting would betray her nervousness to the gimlet-eyed female at the nearby desk.

Though the warm lines of her mouth hinted at character and wit, and her clear eyes held a swift intelligence, at that moment her expressive face was schooled into careful blankness.

She had been regretting her folly for the last twenty-five minutes, and was framing words in her mind, a convincing reason for being unable to wait any longer, when a buzzer made her jump convulsively.

'Mr Cresswell will see you now,' Gerald Baber's secretary announced with cool superiority.

Fighting down a sick panic, Autumn rose to her feet—a slender, long-legged woman with a clear-cut, vivid beauty and glossy, russet-coloured hair—and tapped at the inner door.

'Come in,' a curt voice instructed.

She obeyed and, a few paces inside the literary agent's luxuriously furnished office, was riveted, her green-gold eyes fixed on the man who was standing with his back to her, looking down from the window on to busy Piccadilly.

His imposing height, the width of his shoulders, the arrogant tilt of his dark head, his stance—legs a little apart, hands thrust deep into his pockets—she knew of old.

She also knew that his physical strength was matched by a powerful intellect, a rapier-sharp brain that made him doubly formidable and caused many a lesser man to appear slow and lacking in perception.

He swung round to face her with a suddenness that startled her, making her heart lurch and her breath catch audibly.

That lean, strong-boned face, the winged curve of those almost black brows, the wide mouth with its fuller lower lip, and the slight cleft in the squarish chin, were achingly familiar. Only the glasses, with their thin black metal frames and tinted lenses, were strange and alien.

She had been used to seeing him casually dressed, his T-shirts and jeans often old and stained with blobs of paint, but now he was wearing a charcoal-grey, well-cut business suit with a smart blue shirt and toning tie.

The civilised garb did nothing to disguise his primitive maleness, but in some strange way seemed to accentuate it.

As she stood gazing raptly at him, her heart swelling until it felt like bursting, her slanting eyes filled with tears; tears that overflowed and ran in two silent, unheeded streams down her cheeks and dripped off her chin.

This was the man who had enriched her life, encouraged her talents and stretched her mind. The man who, just by being there, had embroidered the everyday fabric of her existence, making it a rare and beautiful tapestry.

He was also the one who had torn it to shreds.

No, that wasn't true. *She* was the one who had, through her own stupidity, almost destroyed both their lives.

'Good afternoon, Miss Shandon?' His voice, deep and

attractive, just how she recalled it, held a faint note of query.

Autumn's throat worked, but no sound came.

He walked towards the desk with a sureness that made it clear he was well-acquainted with his borrowed surroundings.

Her nerve failing, she half turned to escape.

'Please, sit down.' Though politely phrased, it was an order, issued by a man who was used to giving orders with that casual authority.

She hesitated, stomach churning, estimating the distance between herself and the door, oddly convinced that, despite his disability, if she tried to reach it he would somehow be there before her, barring her way.

'But first, let me take your coat.' Suddenly he was advancing on her with an accuracy that made it difficult to believe he couldn't see.

His hand touched her upper arm, sending a shock-wave through her entire body. A moment later, her smooth fall of below-shoulder-length hair brushing his knuckles, he divested her of the unbuttoned stone-coloured mac she wore, and hung it on a stand.

Somehow her shaky legs carried her the yard or so to a brown leather chair set in front of the mahogany desk. Sitting down, she smoothed the skirt of her Bloomingdale's suit over her knees, almost as if he could see her.

As soon as she was settled he took his own seat behind the desk. Hands clasped together, long fingers interlocked, elbows on the arms of the chair, he leaned back and, swivelling slightly from side to side, asked, 'Quite comfortable, I hope?'

Unnerved by the way he appeared to be looking straight at her, her tongue clove to the roof of her mouth.

When five or six seconds had ticked away, he queried drily, 'I take it the inability to speak isn't permanent? I did stipulate someone quiet, not given to chattering, but *some* communication will be necessary.'

She swallowed and managed huskily, 'I'm sorry, I'm a bit nervous.'

'Of what?' he demanded. 'Being interviewed by a blind man?'

'Of course not.' She was genuinely shocked. 'It's just that I...'

'Do go on,' he urged, when she faltered to a halt.

'I need the job.' It was the very last thing she'd meant to say.

'Then you won't mind answering some questions?'

In her obsession, she hadn't really looked any further than just seeing him again, telling herself that when she'd achieved that end she could make some excuse and leave.

Now, wits scattered, lacking the necessary pluck simply to get up and walk out—if her weak knees would carry her—she steeled herself to go through with the interview. 'No, of course not.'

There wasn't *too* great a danger of discovery. She tried to bolster her courage. It was almost four years since he'd heard her voice, and after living in the States for most of that time she'd picked up enough of a twang to disguise her former Oxford-English accent.

'As this meeting has been arranged at very short notice, and I have no curriculum vitae,' he pursued, 'perhaps we can start with the basics. What is your full name?'

'Elizabeth Shandon.' Asked the same question earlier that day, when she'd rung requesting an interview, Autumn had stammered out her own middle name and her mother's maiden name. Now it came pat.

'How old are you?'

'Twenty-two,' she replied truthfully.

'What qualifications have you?'

'A fair knowledge of modern history, particularly the

eighteenth and nineteenth centuries—' it had been one of the qualifications specified '—and after completing a business course at New York's Lonsdale College I've been secretary to Melvin Frost for the past three years.'

'The American crime writer?'

She nodded, then, realising he couldn't see her, substituted, 'Yes.'

'Why did you leave him?'

Brushing back her light half-fringe with an unsteady hand, she stammered, 'I—I wanted to come back to England.'

It was partly true. Though unwilling to leave Melvin— a mild-mannered, middle-aged man—in the lurch, she might have kept vacillating if he hadn't remarried, and his second wife hadn't turned out to be a trained secretary, effectively making Autumn redundant.

'You were born and brought up in England?'

'Yes.' Watching him flex his lean fingers, she noted abstractedly that he wasn't wearing a wedding-ring.

'Where?'

She should have been prepared. But she wasn't. Her wits totally scattered, she hesitated.

He raised a quizzical brow. 'Forgotten?'

'Oakgreen.' A shade wildly, Autumn named the first village on the Thames that came into her head.

'Fairly close to where I live,' he commented idly. 'Do you know Godsend?'

'No.' The denial was too hurried. Too emphatic.

'How long have you been living in America?'

Afraid of his quick mind making the connection, she hesitated before saying, 'Quite a few years.'

He leaned forward a little. 'Why did you go over there?'

'My father was born in New York,' she replied evasively.

'Are your parents still in the States?'

'They're both dead.'

While, tears drying on her cheeks, she'd struggled to parry his questions, Autumn's eyes had been fixed on him unwaveringly, hungry for the sight of him. Hungry for details.

She'd found herself gazing at him with an almost desperate intensity, as though, in this brief time she'd gambled for and won, she had to make up not only for the last four years, but for all the empty years of her life that still stretched ahead.

He was the same, yet not the same.

His thick peat-dark hair was cut shorter, and he looked older—the nine-year age gap between them would make him thirty-one—and even more dangerously attractive.

It must have been cataclysmic for a man of his proud, independent spirit to be deprived of his sight. To have had his chosen career cut short. God knew what trials and frustrations he'd had to face. Yet somehow he'd won through.

There had always been a kind of reserve about him, a dark side that had both scared and fascinated her. Now there was something new in his face, a discipline, a hardness, that contrasted with, and somehow enhanced, the beauty of his silvery-grey long-lashed eyes and firm, yet sensitive mouth.

Or was she just remembering his eyes as they had been? Though he sat only feet away, they were partially hidden by the tinted lenses, and she wasn't able to see them properly.

She felt a sudden sharp fear that they might be *visibly* injured, and knew she couldn't bear it if they were…

All at once becoming aware that he was waiting for an answer to a question she hadn't taken in, she stammered, 'I—I'm sorry…?'

'I asked if you had any ties? A husband? Children?'

'No,' she said baldly.

'A fiancé, perhaps?'

She looked down at her ringless fingers. She had been engaged for a while, but Richard, a handsome, fair-haired charmer who'd sworn he loved her, had left her after a weekend away he'd planned had gone disastrously wrong. 'No...there's no one.'

'How long have you been back in England?'

'I flew into London yesterday.'

'Where are you staying?'

Reluctantly she told him, 'The Regent Hotel.'

On the plane over, the plump, balding businessman occupying the neighbouring seat had been both cheerful and friendly, and they'd talked at length during the long flight.

When Autumn had mentioned that she needed somewhere to stay for a night of two, Mr Davis had suggested that particular hotel, saying he himself was booked in there. They had shared a taxi.

'How did you hear of this post?'

'I read about it in *Top People*.'

Mr Davis had also proffered the magazine, which was open at 'Book News', remarking half jokingly, 'If you're looking for a job, this might be just the ticket.' His blunt forefinger had indicated the relevant paragraphs.

Like someone in a dream, Autumn had read them.

Best-selling author Saul Cresswell has been specially commissioned to write a sequel to his award-winning novel *The Lightning Tree*.

In his younger days Mr Cresswell made a name for himself as a talented artist before turning with equal success to writing. Though his books are acclaimed world-wide, little is known about the man himself. He refuses to be photographed or give interviews, and has a reputation for being

morose and taciturn after a car crash some years ago robbed
him of his sight and turned him into a virtual recluse.

Gerald Baber, Mr Cresswell's agent, informs us that the
author is currently looking for a replacement secretary for
a period of two to three months, but special qualifications
are needed. Any applicant must have a sound knowledge
of modern history, and be prepared to work long hours and
in isolation.

Interested persons should call Mr Baber's Piccadilly office, where possible candidates will be interviewed by Mr
Cresswell…

Autumn had sat staring at the page, her heart thudding
against her ribs. She had felt as if fate had dealt her a body-
blow, yet at the same time offered, like some priceless gift,
a chance to see him again.

A chance she dared not take, because even if *he* was
unable to recognise her, Joanna undoubtedly would.

Apparently he really did keep his private life just that.
There had been no mention of his wife, and, though Joanna
had never seemed the maternal type, it was quite possible
he had children by now.

Perhaps that was why he needed to shut himself away to
write?

Autumn had been living in New York almost six months
when the news of Saul's impending marriage had filtered
through in a letter from a family friend. Eighteen months
later she had heard about the outstanding success of his
first book, *Darkness Be My Friend*.

Deeply thankful that he was starting to put his life together again, she had prayed that all would go well, and
from then on had made a positive effort to let him go, to
cut the ties which, on her side at least, still bound them to
one another.

Without success.

She had tried equally hard to ignore the opportunity that

fate seemed almost to have thrust at her. But like a magnet it had drawn her until she could think of nothing else but the possibility of seeing him again.

The fact that the interviews were to be conducted not at his Thames-side home but at his agent's office greatly reduced the risk of encountering Joanna, and provided a lure that Autumn—after a night of mingled apprehension and longing—had been unable to resist.

In an effort to justify such craziness, she'd told herself that if only she could see him once more she might finally be able to break the invisible bonds that continued to hold her fast.

Four years were bound to make a difference. He wouldn't be the same man, any more than she was the same woman. Seeing him might enable her to bury the past and make a fresh start.

In fear and trembling in case she was too late, she had rung the Piccadilly number, only to be thrown into a maelstrom of nervous excitement when, after being informed that several other people had already been interviewed, she'd been asked to present herself at four o'clock that same afternoon.

It had left little time for saner counsel to prevail...

'Then you're aware that it will mean living in virtual isolation for a couple of months at least?' His brusque voice broke into her thoughts.

Her almond eyes refocusing on his hard face, she answered, 'Yes.'

'And you could start immediately?'

'Yes.'

'Do you drive?'

'Yes...though I'm used to driving on the right.'

'That shouldn't be a problem.' He steepled his fingers, tapping them together. 'I'm prepared to pay a good salary to the right person, say—' he named a sum that was ex-

ceedingly generous '—but whoever takes the job must be
prepared to do some cooking and a little light housework.'

'But won't your wife—?' She stopped abruptly.

His head came up, and behind the dark glasses his eyes
seemed to narrow. 'What makes you so sure I'm married?'

'Well, I—I'm not sure.' She ran an agitated hand through
her silky fringe. 'I just thought you'd have someone to run
your home.'

'When I'm writing to a deadline I don't work at home.
I need total concentration. To make sure I'm not disturbed,
I go to my house on the North Yorkshire moors, where no
one, not èven my agent or my publisher, can reach me.'

'Oh,' she said faintly.

'Does that worry you?'

'No.' As she had very little chance of being offered the
job and no intention whatsoever of taking it...

Without warning he rose to his feet and moved round
the desk to stand just slightly to one side of her.

Startled into immobility, she stared up at him as though
mesmerised, her breath coming fast.

'As I have no idea what you look like—all I know is
that your hair smells of apple-blossom—would you mind
if I...?'

His hands were already travelling unerringly towards her
face when she flinched away, exclaiming, 'No! No, I'd
rather you didn't...'

The movement stopped and his hands—long, well-
shaped artist's hands—dropped to his sides.

Catching her panic by the coat-tails, she managed breath-
lessly, 'I—I'm sorry, Mr Cresswell. I didn't mean to react
so violently. But I dislike being touched.'

'In that case,' he said evenly, 'perhaps you'll describe
yourself? Your colouring, how tall you are...'

Almost five feet eight inches tall by the time she'd
reached her teens, half a head taller than most of her

friends, Autumn had been terribly self-conscious about her height. Only Saul, at six feet four inches, had towered over her, making her feel small and feminine. She'd had to tilt her long, graceful neck just to look at him.

Afraid her true height might strike a chord, she took two inches off. 'I'm five feet six, about one hundred and thirty pounds...' She was safe telling him that. When he'd seen her last she had weighed a good fifteen pounds more.

Now came the difficult part. Her parents had chosen her name for more than one reason. She had been born in the autumn of their lives, her birthday was on the last day of September, and she had autumn colouring.

Give-away colouring.

Reminding herself that he couldn't see, she lied, 'Brownish hair and eyes.'

'Very comprehensive,' he commented sarcastically. Then, like a whiplash, 'Why are you so frightened?'

'I'm not,' she denied.

'Do you think that because I can't see, I'm completely in the dark about what goes on?'

When she didn't answer, he said with a kind of soft menace, 'Being without one sense hones the others. I can hear the slightest change in your breathing, every catch in your voice—' his long fingers located and lightly encircled her wrist, before slipping down to touch her hand '—feel that your pulse is racing and your palms are clammy. You've been scared stiff ever since you walked in. Earlier you were crying. Why?'

His nearness, his touch, and the certain knowledge of how he would react if he knew it was her, made Autumn feel faint.

Like a single dark strand plaited into a golden cord, her love had always had a thread of fear.

She glanced at the door in desperation, but he was effectively barring her way. 'I—I told you. I was nervous about the job.'

'You must want it very badly.' It was a statement, not a question, but still he paused, as though waiting for her assurance that she did.

'Well, yes, I…'

'Then it's yours.'

She knew he must have heard and noted the hiss of her indrawn breath. 'I—I don't understand why you're offering it to me,' she faltered.

'As well as having the necessary qualifications, you seem to need personal space. Anyone who does usually respects other people's. You don't strike me as the sort of woman who would want to stir my coffee, or who would regard me as being helpless. Because one of my senses is impaired I find it intolerable to be fussed over, or treated as though I was mentally defective…'

'Oh, surely…' The start of an instinctive protest was torn from her.

'Believe me, it happens,' he assured her grimly. 'Before I realised the advantages of relative solitude I allowed my then fiancée to persuade me to take tea with a friend of hers. My hostess asked, "Does he take sugar?" as though I was incapable of answering for myself.

'Thoroughly mortified, I lost my cool and rushed out, stumbling into furniture and things I hadn't noted were there. I swore to myself it would never happen again…'

For the first time Autumn glimpsed the searing bitterness that lay beneath his veneer of imperturbability, and her heart ached for him.

'However, that's all in the past.' Smoothly he added, 'I'm quite sure we'll suit one another and work well together.'

Iron bands tightening around her chest, she began, 'Oh, but I don't…' The words tailed away. With him looming over her there was no way she could now admit to not wanting the job.

He sucked in a breath, hollowing his cheeks. 'Don't what, Miss Shandon?'

'I—I don't have any actual references.'

His laugh was harsh, mirthless. 'I couldn't read them if you had. And in this instance I prefer to rely on my instincts... You said you could start immediately, so if you can be ready to travel to Yorkshire tomorrow morning?'

She must agree to whatever he suggested, Autumn decided desperately, then as soon as she had got away from Mr Baber's office she could ring up and say she'd changed her mind.

But, without waiting for her answer, Saul was going on, 'My car will be at the hotel by ten o'clock. You can handle a Rover?'

When she made a muffled sound that could have been assent, he added, 'Then you can drive us up to Feldon. Not only will it save George having to make a return journey, but it will mean we have transport from Farthing Beck should we need it.'

He touched his fingers to his left wrist, where he wore a Braille watch. 'How are you getting back to your hotel?'

'I'm going on the subway.'

'You'll hit the rush-hour. If you wait a few minutes, I'm being picked up. We can drop you.'

It might be Joanna coming to fetch him. Jumping to her feet, scarcely able to keep the panic out of her voice, Autumn said, 'Thank you, but I'm quite used to coping with New York's rush-hour.'

Shrugging slightly, he reached for her mac and, without a single fumble, held it so that she could slip her arms into the sleeves.

Unnerved by his very sureness, she pulled it on and

moved hurriedly away, leaving several feet of space between them.

Standing where he was, he held out his hand.

Her heart thumping so loudly that she felt sure he must
hear, she put hers into it. When she withdrew it, though his
clasp had been light, she nursed it with her other hand as
though it had suffered some injury.

Stepping to the door, he opened it politely. 'Until tomorrow, then, Miss Shandon.'

'Goodnight.' Slipping past him, she fairly fled across the
now empty outer office and, trembling in every limb, took
the lift down to the ground floor where the last straggling
groups of the nine-to-five brigade were just leaving.

Not until she was well clear of the building, and safe
from the possibility of running into Joanna, did she breathe
a little easier.

It was a cold, drizzly, late November evening, already
dark, the lights of Piccadilly gleaming on the bustling traffic and the wet pavements, as she joined the throng of pe-
destrians heading for the nearest tube station.

Strap-hanging on the crowded train, she kept asking herself if it had been worth the trauma, the grief and heart-
break of seeing Saul as he was now.

Had it solved anything?

Hoping against hope that she'd look at him and find she
no longer cared, she'd looked at him and found she cared
a thousand times more.

She had prayed that her feelings for him might have died
and she could bury them. They hadn't died, and how could
you bury something that was still living?

No, it had solved nothing.

Yet just to see him again had been worth everything.

As soon as she reached the hotel she crossed the foyer
to the public telephones, and was about to dial Mr Baber's

number when she paused. Everyone would have gone home. She would be speaking to an answering-machine.

It made more sense to leave her call until tomorrow morning. That way it would look as though she'd taken a night to think about it and change her mind. So long as she phoned in plenty of time for them to get in touch with him and prevent him setting out…

Even so, he would be angry. He had settled everything to his satisfaction, and he wasn't a man to suffer fools gladly, or tolerate having his plans thwarted. And if he should have the faintest suspicion that Elizabeth Shandon was in reality Autumn Milski…

Shivering, she made up her mind to check out of the hotel as soon as she'd phoned. Though it wasn't likely he'd come looking for her, she'd feel a great deal safer if she was somewhere else.

In any case, she would need to move to cheaper accommodation while she endeavoured to find a job and a bed-sit.

Not basically a city person, she would have liked to go back to Godsend, where she had spent her teenage years. In many ways, idyllic years. But through her own stupidity she had made that impossible. There was too much shame and guilt, too many memories to flay her, even if Saul hadn't still been living there.

Her father—born in the United States, of Polish descent—and her mother—Scottish as the banks and braes of bonnie Doon—had both been musicians: blond Daniel Milski a highly respected conductor; black-haired Katrine Shandon a virtuoso violinist.

Cecilia Cottage, a charming, black and white half-timbered house, their home for five years, had been dedicated to music.

Autumn had dearly loved the old place, but now she dared not so much as pay it a flying visit.

In London she could easily get lost in the crowd, but in a small town like Godsend she might run into people who would recognise her. And the very last thing she wanted was for Saul to hear she was back...

After eating a solitary meal at a nearby snack-bar, she decided on an early night. But, tired as she was, thoughts of Saul, images of his dark face, made her sleep restless.

She awoke heavy-eyed and headachy to find morning mist swirling against the windows and veiling the traffic.

It was just after seven o'clock. Plenty of time to make that phone call...as soon as she'd decided exactly what to say.

An electric kettle had been provided, and by the time she'd made and drank a cup of coffee she had hit on the only excuse that might sound feasible. She must say that she'd changed her mind about staying in England, and had decided to return to the States.

Having showered, she dressed in a moss-green suit that echoed the colour of her eyes, repacked her case and hand-grip and, gathering up her shoulder-bag and mac, made her way down to Reception.

When she had paid her bill and checked out, she asked, 'Can I leave my belongings at the side here while I make a telephone call?'

'Certainly, Miss Shandon.' The desk-clerk was a young, sallow-faced man, brisk and efficient. 'But if it's a taxi you want...?'

Autumn shook her head. Apart from the fact that she hadn't yet decided where she was going, taxi-fares were a luxury she wasn't sure she could afford.

'Then I'll keep a sharp eye on your things,' he promised.

It was barely eight-thirty and Mr Baber's answering-machine was still switched on. As concisely and convincingly as possible, she made her excuses and apologies, stressing the need to ring Mr Cresswell without delay.

The foyer was busy with people coming to and going from the breakfast-room. As she made her way past the glass doors the appetising smell of bacon brought a hunger-pang and made her mouth water.

Knowing it would be considerably cheaper to buy a bacon sandwich at the snack-bar, she resisted the temptation.

And, even more important, she had to be well away from the hotel before ten o'clock, just in case there was any slip-up in communicating her decision to Saul.

As she edged through a group of businessmen the desk-clerk spotted her bright head and, straightening, said, 'Ah, Miss Shandon, there's a gentleman asking for you.'

The only person she knew in London was the man she had sat next to on the plane. Now, what was his name? Ah, yes, Davis...

A polite smile forming on her lips, she turned in the direction the desk-clerk was indicating.

Instead of the short, balding, innocuous individual she'd been expecting, there was a tall, dark, tough-looking man wearing tinted glasses.

It was like walking slap into a steel shutter.

CHAPTER TWO

'GOOD MORNING.' Saul Cresswell held out his hand. Though reeling from the shock, she automatically took it, and felt those lean fingers close around hers in a light, but somehow relentless grip.

'I decided on a slight change of plan—' once again he appeared to be looking straight at her '—for which, by some lucky chance, your timing is impeccable. You've checked out, I understand, but you haven't breakfasted yet?'

'Y-yes… No…' Stammering, totally thrown, her heart racing, her breathing hampered by a mixture of fierce joy at seeing him again and an equally powerful apprehension, she scarcely knew what she was saying.

Releasing her hand, he went on, 'As you will be driving, it occurred to me that it would be better if we had breakfast together and discussed the route before we make a start.'

Taking her agreement for granted, he addressed the grizzled, thick-set man standing alongside. 'If you'll just put Miss Shandon's things in the boot of the car, please, George? And leave the back window down a few inches.'

'Very good, sir,' George answered. Gathering up Autumn's luggage with speedy efficiency, he made for the door.

'Oh, but I…' Far too late, she tried to collect her wits and repeat what she'd already put on record.

Seeing her concern, and obviously mistaking the cause,

Saul said reassuringly, 'There's no need to worry. The Rover is child's play to handle.'

George was back in seconds. Handing Saul the car keys, he said, as though he rather doubted it, 'I hope you have a safe journey.'

'Don't worry.' As the man turned to go Saul clapped him on the back, and added, a shade drily, 'I'm sure we can both leave everything in my new secretary's capable hands...and they are capable.' Picking up her right hand once more, Saul tucked it through his arm and imprisoned it there. His voice soft and deep, oddly intimate, he went on, 'Long-fingered, slender and shapely, yet strong. Pianist's hands, perhaps?'

'No!' Autumn said sharply. But even as the denial crossed her lips she recalled those long-ago evenings when, with both parents pursuing their individual careers, she had played for hours, with Saul a silent, contented listener.

A sudden suspicion that somehow he'd guessed made her blood run cold. But, with a casual shrug, he said merely, 'That's a pity... Now, shall we see about some breakfast?'

This morning he was casually dressed in beige trousers, a navy-blue roll-neck sweater, and an unzipped corduroy jacket. He looked handsomer than ever.

As he walked easily by her side she marvelled at his quiet confidence. Hard-won confidence, no doubt.

There was a table for two by the door. Pulling herself together, she suggested, 'Shall we sit here?'

He waited until she was settled, then, slipping off his jacket, he hung it on the back of the chair and took his own seat.

Almost immediately a waiter was at his elbow, turning the page on his pad, pencil at the ready.

Head very slightly cocked, finely tuned hearing evidently taking the place of sight, Saul asked Autumn, 'What would you like?'

'I—I'm not really hungry.' Her earlier appetite had vanished completely.

Without further ado he ordered coffee and croissants for them both and, when the waiter had moved away, began in a businesslike voice to discuss their route north.

'There's a map in the car you can look at later, but I think the A1 is our best option. If we go...'

Only half listening, she tried frantically to think of some way out of this impossible situation. Of course, the simplest thing would be to *tell* him...

Unable to drum up the courage to admit she had no intention of going anywhere with him, she cravenly considered the idea of simply getting up and walking out.

But she couldn't bring herself just to leave him sitting there... Perhaps if she asked one of the waiters to give him a message as soon as she was gone...?

About to rise, it suddenly dawned on her that all her belongings were locked in his car. She was absorbing that unpleasant jolt when his dry question penetrated her abstraction.

'I believe at the interview I mentioned the need for *some* communication, Miss Shandon?'

'Yes, I—I'm sorry, Mr Cresswell. Did you...?'

'I asked if you were happy with the proposed route?'

'Well, yes...I...'

'It's quite straightforward. Shortly after Rainton we leave the A1 and head east for Hutton-le-Hole and the moors...'

At that moment their breakfast arrived, the waiter unloading the tray with speed and efficiency.

Having handed him a note, Saul waved away the change.

'Shall I pour your coffee?' Autumn asked, a shade hesitantly.

Behind the tinted glasses she saw the gleam of his eyes before he answered blandly, 'Please do.'

Though the rest of the day he took it black and sugarless,

she knew he had liked his breakfast coffee with hot milk
and a little brown sugar. Wary, however, of revealing that
knowledge, and respecting his wish not to be fussed over,
she deliberately left it black.

Setting it down by his plate with a faint rattle, to make
sure he could locate it, she put the jug of hot milk and the
sugar-basin slightly to the right.

'Thank you.' With wry mockery, he added, 'That was
done with skill and no little tact.'

His lean fingers travelled lightly up the cup to judge the
depth of coffee, before he neatly and competently helped
himself to milk and a small amount of sugar.

The croissants were warm and flaky and smelled so good
that Autumn's hunger suddenly returned. Having taken one,
she selected a container of strawberry jam, and was making
her fourth attempt to peel back the top when Saul queried,
'Having trouble?'

'I never can get into these little plastic containers,' she
grumbled.

Holding out his hand, he said, 'Let me.'

A second later it was open and, wrinkling his nose, he
was passing it back.

As she thanked him he said, 'Now you can do something
for me. Find one that isn't strawberry.'

Saul had always disliked strawberry jam, preferring a
tarter fruit.

'There's your favourite, blackcurrant,' she said.

'Have you always had psychic powers?' he asked
gravely.

Her heart lurched sickeningly. 'Wh-what?'

His face satirical above the navy-blue roll-neck sweater,
he queried, 'How do you know blackcurrant is my favourite?'

'I—I don't, of course. I'm sorry, I must have been thinking of Richard.'

'Who's Richard?'

'My ex-fiancé.'

He gave a little grunt, as though satisfied, and began to eat his croissant.

Still she cursed herself for a fool. If she was going to Yorkshire with him she would need to be a great deal more careful. On her guard not to make stupid mistakes...

But she wasn't going to Yorkshire with him. How could she even contemplate such a thing? It would be the height of lunacy. As reckless as playing Russian roulette with a loaded revolver.

But, oh, dear God, how she *wanted* to.

He was back in her veins like a virus to which she had lost, or rather had never had, any immunity.

Two or three months alone with him... To hear his voice, to see him every day, to work by his side. It would be worth selling her soul, her place in paradise for...

She visualised a heavenly auction, the angel Gabriel asking, 'How much will you give for this unique opportunity?'

Herself saying, 'Everything I have.'

No! No, she mustn't do it. If Saul discovered who she was... She shivered, remembering things she would rather have forgotten. Remembering how, on that September night four years ago, she had set in motion the train of events that were subsequently to wreck his life.

Although shocked and furious, he had managed to keep control, barely raising his voice to her, though he had made his anger and contempt quite plain.

Still, she hadn't learnt her lesson. Her deliberate provocation had pushed him over the edge, making him lose that control and behave in a way he would later regret.

'Now get out, you silly little fool!' he'd said, with a kind of raging calm. 'Go on, run! Get out of my life and stay out. If I ever set eyes on you again we might both be sorry.'

So she had run.

The next day, knowing she couldn't live with herself until she'd at least tried to put things right, Autumn had gone to see Joanna, to tell her the truth.

It had been a traumatic experience in every way. Having flayed the younger girl mercilessly, Joanna had told her about the car crash, laying the blame squarely on Autumn's shoulders.

Love proving stronger than fear, she had hurried to the hospital and pleaded to be allowed to see Saul, but the doctor had decreed no visitors.

For three days and nights she had haunted the infirmary, and as soon as he was out of Intensive Care she had tried again, desperate just to *see* him, to tell him how sorry she was for what she'd done, to beg his forgiveness.

The stern, grey-haired sister in charge of Harry Duncton Ward had said he didn't want to see her.

While still reeling from that blow, she had been told he'd lost his sight.

She'd wanted to die.

Through her, Saul had lost everything, including his career.

Later the same day, she had tried again, begging hoarsely, 'Oh, please, *please* let me see him, if it's only for a minute...'

Bony face implacable, the sister had refused, saying, 'I've been asked not to allow you in.'

'But if he's alone...'

'Mr Cresswell isn't alone. His fiancée is by his side.'

The fact that Joanna was with him, and the knowledge that, being from a wealthy background, he shouldn't *need* to work, had been the only faint gleams of light in the blackness.

A few weeks later, when her father was due to take up the post of conductor to the New World Symphony

Orchestra, Autumn, numb with misery, had moved to the
States with her parents.

Delighted by her change of heart, her unexpected decision to go with them, they had never questioned her mo-
tives.

During the following months, her thoughts always with
Saul, she had started slowly and painfully to try and patch
up her own life.

After a couple of years she had almost convinced herself
that she'd succeeded. But beneath her composure, her veneer of happiness, guilt, regret, sadness, and a restless,
gnawing emptiness, had lurked like sharks.

Then, a few months ago, her parents had died within
weeks of each other. Their deaths had been followed by
the loss of both her fiancé and her job. Notice to quit her
furnished apartment had been the final blow, bringing the
sharks to the surface and driving her back to England.

Back to Saul and this strange predicament...

Sighing, she finished her coffee and put her cup down
on the saucer.

'About ready?' He pushed back his chair and got up with
the quick, athletic grace she knew of old. 'It's a fair way,
and I'd like to be there well before it's dark.'

But having risen obediently, automatically, she stood
quite still, hesitating, unsure of either what to do or what
to say.

Pulling on his jacket, he asked crisply, 'Not getting cold
feet, are you?'

She must tell him she was. Tell him she'd changed her
mind.

'Cold feet?' Her voice sounded thick and impeded.

'At the idea of being alone for weeks on end with a blind
man?'

She couldn't let him think that. Lifting her chin, she demanded, 'What possible difference could your being blind make?'

His powerful shoulders lifted in a slight shrug. 'As you said how much you wanted the job, and now you're hesitating, that's the only inference I can draw.'

'It happens to be the wrong one, Mr Cresswell.' She spoke curtly.

Through the tinted glasses she saw the gleam of his eyes. 'Then let's go.'

With a strange feeling of fatality she let him tuck her hand beneath his elbow, and together they left the dining-room and crossed the foyer.

When they reached the main doors a crush of people made it impossible to remain side by side. Dropping back, Saul walked a little behind her, one hand at her waist, the fingers of his other hand lightly encircling her wrist.

She wondered if he could hear the rapidity of her breathing, feel her pulse racing.

'You'll see a maroon Rover on the forecourt to your left,' he told her as they descended the steps.

When they reached the car he produced the keys and unlocked it, stooping to speak to someone inside.

Autumn heard the name Beth, and at the same time caught a glimpse of a large furry head and pricked ears, a plume of a tail waving.

So that was why he had asked for one of the windows to be left down.

Still imprisoning her wrist—as though he thought she might change her mind and make a run for it—Saul opened the car door, only releasing her as she slid behind the wheel.

A moment later he had walked round the bonnet and was taking his place in the front passenger seat.

'I hope you haven't an aversion to dogs?' he asked as

he handed her the keys. 'It was the one thing I forgot to ask.'

'No...no, I haven't. I like animals.' Aware that she sounded breathless, she turned to look at the beautiful fawn and black Alsatian bitch stretched full length on the back seat.

'Beth has been with me over three years now,' Saul remarked. 'She's a fully trained guide dog, though these days she doesn't wear a harness.'

His tone becoming brisker, more businesslike, he added, 'There's a map in the door-pocket if you want to consult it before we start.'

After a glance at the map, a few minor adjustments to the seat and mirrors, and a reminder to herself to stay on the left, Autumn turned the key in the ignition.

The car proved to be a dream to drive, and once clear of London they made good time.

While they'd breakfasted the sun had burnt a hole in the mist, and by mid-morning the November day was clear and bright.

During the journey, Saul sat quiet and relaxed, making no attempt at conversation, while Autumn drove mechanically, busy with her thoughts.

Uneasy thoughts.

She was behaving like a mad fool, leaving herself wide open to God knew what if he should discover who she was.

He wasn't the kind of man to forgive. And he certainly couldn't forget. Probably nothing would give him greater pleasure than to flay her alive.

But having accepted the fact that each day spent in his company would be dangerous, still she knew that where *he* was seemed like home, and there was nowhere in the world she would rather be.

Towards lunchtime, at Saul's suggestion, they stopped at

a wayside inn for a snack and to let Beth stretch her legs
and have a drink.

She was big for a bitch, with a glossy coat and calm,
intelligent eyes. Ignoring everything, including a small
black dog which escaped from its owner and came yapping
at her heels, she walked by her master's side, giving him
her undivided attention.

The lounge of the Drunken Duck was cheerful and
homely, and practically empty.

Sitting in front of a blazing fire, the dog at their feet,
they shared a plate of roast-beef sandwiches. Then, while
Saul finished his glass of bitter, Autumn had a cup of coffee.

Seeing him check his watch, she said, 'I'd like to wash
my hands before we start.'

'This is where George would have come in handy,' Saul
remarked wryly.

Refusing to allow the slightest trace of embarrassment to
creep into her voice, she suggested, 'If we go together, the
washrooms are usually side by side.'

'What a very practical solution.' His tone was lightly
mocking.

As soon as he began to rise, Beth was on her feet, alert
and waiting. She accompanied them out of the bar and
along a corridor.

'Here we are,' Autumn said matter-of-factly. 'The gen-
tlemen's washroom is straight ahead.'

As she disappeared into the ladies' she heard Saul give
the bitch a quiet command.

When, having freshened up and run a comb through her
long, glossy hair, she made her way out, Beth was stretched
full length, effectively blocking the narrow space.

Not wanting to be found hovering in the corridor like
some too-zealous guardian, Autumn attempted to pass. The

bitch gave a low growl, and lifted her lip to display gleaming white fangs.

'It's all right, Beth,' Autumn said firmly. 'You can wait
for him, but I'm going back.'

The animal would have none of it. Hackles up, she repeated the warning.

Though unafraid of dogs, Autumn knew when she'd met
her match.

A few moments later Saul appeared. The bitch immediately got up and put her nose to his hand. He fondled her
ears.

'I'm afraid Beth refused to let me pass,' Autumn remarked, making light of it.

'Ah...' he murmured, with a soft satisfaction that made
her half suspect he had ordered the bitch to keep her there.
'Perhaps she thought you might be going to run off without
me,' he added jokingly.

Or was he joking? Autumn wondered as they made their
way back to the car. *She* had locked the Rover and put the
keys in her bag. Had he been making sure she wouldn't try
to escape while his back was turned?

Escape. It was a very emotive word. Her heart began to
thud against her ribcage. Recalling his early arrival at the
hotel, the way he'd immediately had her luggage locked in
his car, how his lean fingers had encircled her wrist until
she was behind the wheel, she felt cold shivers of apprehension crawl up and down her spine.

Taking a grip, she told herself sternly not to be a melodramatic idiot. She wouldn't have read anything remotely
sinister into his actions if she hadn't had a guilty conscience.

But suppose he'd guessed who she was?

Of course he hadn't guessed; her common sense pooh-
poohed the idea. If he'd had the faintest suspicion, he

would have sent her packing immediately, not offered her the job.

Still, she found herself reluctant to get back in the car. Hesitating, the keys in her hand, the chill wind ruffling her wispy fringe, she wondered what he would do if she made a run for it. Send Beth after her, probably…

Oh, really! she scolded herself crossly. With that kind of unbridled imagination, she could be writing plots for cheap thrillers.

Sighing at her own stupidity, she unlocked the car and, while Saul settled the dog in the back, slipped behind the wheel. He slammed her door, and a moment later slid in beside her.

There was no turning back now. Perhaps there never had been. Suddenly she shivered.

They left the inn behind them and continued their journey, and, wanting to get on a steadier, more mundane, footing, Autumn asked, 'How big is your house, Mr Cresswell?'

'Fairly large.' His tone was reassuringly pleasant and friendly. 'Farthing Beck was originally an old manor-cum-farm.'

'How long have you had it?'

'About three years. It was willed to me by my godfather. Mr and Mrs Skipton, who run the local inn, take care of the place while I'm not there. They have a Land Rover so they can reach it in all but the worst weather. When I intend coming I let them know and they start the generator, stock the freezer, and lay in a store of wood for me…'

By the time they had left the A1 and headed through the hills into the North Yorkshire moors, the bright afternoon had clouded over and skeins of dark cloud were unravelling themselves threateningly.

'It looks as if it might be going to rain, or possibly snow,' Autumn remarked, a shade uneasily.

'They quite often have early snow on the moors,' he told her, adding casually, 'In this kind of terrain, heavy drifting means that Farthing Beck sometimes gets cut off for days at a time.'

Anything but reassured, she relapsed into silence.

Following a narrow ribbon of road, they travelled for what seemed endless miles without seeing anything but shaggy grey sheep and an occasional isolated farm.

Awed by the desolate grandeur of the wild moors, realising, perhaps for the first time, just what she'd let herself in for, Autumn was growing even more uneasy, when Saul remarked, 'We should soon be reaching Feldon. It's a hamlet made up of a dozen or so farms and cottages, a store and garage combined, and the Green Man inn....'

As he spoke they breasted a rise and below them, in a shallow depression, a cluster of buildings came into view.

Grey and bleak, huddled together for protection, the only sign of life or movement was smoke swirling from one of the chimneys, a black and white sheep-dog moving with that breed's peculiar slinking gait, and the inn-sign swinging a little in the rising wind.

'A couple of hundred yards beyond the Green Man we turn left and take a track that runs across the moors to Farthing Beck, the brook the original house was named after...'

They had bumped along the rough track for the best part of two miles when the place came into view. Long and low and rambling, substantially built of grey stone, it had a hotchpotch of gables and squat chimneys. Behind, and to the left, were the remains of some farm buildings.

It lay on the far side of a wide, shallow brook. Only sheep-cropped grass, several bare, stunted thorn-trees, and a solitary pine separated it from the moor.

Autumn drove across the old hump-backed bridge with

care and stopped on the cobbled area to one side of the entrance.

Handing her a large ornate key, Saul said, 'Perhaps you would be kind enough to open the door?'

By the time she had turned the key in the lock, he, with the dog by his side, was lifting their luggage from the boot.

The heavy oak door opened straight into a black-beamed combined kitchen and living-room with a smooth, flagged floor strewn with bright rugs.

Heated by a huge, solid-fuel stove, the place felt comfortably warm, the fire glowing cheerfully behind glass doors. On either side of the stove, neat piles of logs were stacked in the recesses.

While Saul disposed of their baggage, Autumn looked around. The large room was simply but adequately furnished, with a three-piece suite set around a low table, a dining-table and chairs, and a standard-lamp. A music centre stood beneath the window, and close by there was a desk with a covered typewriter and battery-powered tape recorder. All the rest of the wall was taken up by bookshelves.

The sight brought a lump to her throat. Saul had once shared her love of reading and they had wrangled amiably over their best-loved authors...

'I find it easier to use just the one room.' His voice at her elbow made her jump.

Glad he couldn't see the convulsive movement, she swallowed, and asked, 'Who usually comes with you?'

'George. But, though he's useful in many ways, his cooking leaves a lot to be desired... Now, if I show you your room...'

While Beth settled herself in front of the stove, Saul, with a confidence that proved he was on home ground, led the way along a passage, through an inner hall, where a small round table held a glass-chimneyed oil lamp, and up the oak stairs.

'There are seven bedrooms,' he went on, 'but only the two we're going to be using are furnished.'

To the left of the broad landing, he pushed open a door already ajar.

The large, whitewashed room was sparsely furnished with a bow-fronted chest of drawers and a heavy, old-fashioned bedstead and wardrobe. Faded rugs were scattered on the polished black floorboards.

Set in the thick walls were mullioned windows which looked out across the beck to the dark moors. An oil-lamp, a twin to the one downstairs, stood on the wide sill, and beside it a box of matches and a candle in a black metal holder.

Her belongings, she saw, had been placed on a carved wooden blanket-box to one side of a small blackleaded fireplace.

There was no heating and the air was distinctly chill.

When she failed to comment, he queried, his face sardonic, 'I hope you weren't anticipating frills?'

'No, I wasn't,' she answered evenly.

'Then I'll leave you to get settled in... By the way, the bathroom's opposite.'

'An unexpected luxury.' She made no attempt to hide the irony. 'How nice.'

With the dry humour she remembered of old, he informed her, 'You won't think so if the pump becomes temperamental while you're in the middle of a shower.'

At the door he turned to say, 'Beth needs a walk, so when I've changed into something warmer, I'm going to stretch my legs.' An odd nuance in his voice, he added, 'I always think better on the move.'

'Oh, but will you...?' With an effort she bit back the

hasty words of concern. He surely must know what he was doing.

His beautiful mouth took on a derisive slant, but all he said was, 'I'll show you round the rest of the house tomorrow.'

Shivering a little, Autumn changed her suit for donkey-brown trousers and a cream sweater before unpacking the rest of her things.

Her emotions were turbulent, swinging like a weather-vane in a changing wind. Panicky excitement that she was actually here. A disquieting feeling of guilt, when she thought what Joanna's reaction would be. Joy at being with Saul. Fear that he might suspect who she really was...

Already he'd guessed that she was a pianist...and then she'd made that slip over the jam...

In an effort to minimise the danger, she told herself bracingly that so long as she was careful not to make any more idiotic mistakes, once he was absorbed in his work there would be far less risk.

By the time she'd put away her clothes and placed her toilet things in the antiquated bathroom, a grey dusk was creeping stealthily out of hiding to shroud the rolling moors and press against the panes.

Saul was out somewhere in that bleak wilderness, and it would soon be dark...

But darkness would make no difference to him. The thought, intended to be comforting, hurt like a knife-thrust.

The old house was quiet, almost eerily so, as she made her way through the gloom to the living-room, and she became conscious of a faint hum, which after a moment she realised was probably the generator.

Feeling decidedly jumpy, ill at ease, she touched a switch and wall-lights came on, bringing a reassuring normality.

Determinedly turning her thoughts to practicalities, she looked around the kitchen area. It was neat and clean but basic, with a stainless-steel sink, a washing machine, a small oven and a microwave.

An airing cupboard held a hot-water tank with an immersion heater and a pump. The heater had been switched on.

In the far corner was a tall fridge-freezer, with what appeared to be a good selection of fresh food, a stack of ready-cooked meals, and a cold drawer full of various bottles.

Next to it was a storage cabinet with several shelves of groceries and tinned food. There was also a medicine chest on the wall. A necessity no doubt in such an isolated place.

Autumn made herself a cup of tea and, when she'd drunk it, began to prepare an evening meal, all the while wondering where Saul had got to, listening anxiously for his return.

The frightening thought that something might have happened to him popped into her head and refused to go away.

Suppose he'd somehow got lost? No, no, Beth would bring him home safely. If he could walk… But what if he'd twisted his ankle in one of the many pot-holes that littered the track…?

Oh, for goodness' sake! He certainly wouldn't thank her for reacting like an over-anxious mother.

Still, if he wasn't back soon she would risk his wrath and take the car to look for him.

Take the car…

But where were the keys? She'd meant to put them in her bag as a safety measure, just in case she had to make a run for it, but somehow she'd forgotten.

A moment's thought convinced her they must still be in the ignition. When Saul had handed her the house key and asked her to open the door, she had got straight out to do his bidding.

It was a pitch-black, moonless night, and she shivered in

the bitter wind as she hurried over to the car. Opening the door she reached inside.

The ignition was empty.

Her mouth went dry and her heart started to thud against her ribs. Saul must have taken the keys.

So what had he done with them?

Suddenly it was vitally important that she should find them—on more than one count.

A hurried search of the kitchen proved unsuccessful. Perhaps he'd left them in his bedroom?

Strangely unwilling to turn her back on the warm, cheerful room, she used her will-power like a whip to drive herself into the chill gloom of the passage.

Unable to locate the light-switches, she fumbled her way across the hall and up the stairs, hemmed in by an all-enveloping darkness.

She had reached the landing when, with a most unpleasant shock, she recalled the oil-lamps on the hall table and on her windowsill, and realised there was no electricity beyond the living-room.

Gritting her teeth, she felt for her bedroom door and opened it. The windows showed up faintly as black rectangles against the deeper blackness.

Slow and shuffling, hands stretched ahead, she moved hesitantly towards them, one of the sloping floorboards creaking beneath her feet.

After what seemed an age she touched the stone sill and began to search for the matchbox she knew was there. It rattled as, fingers far from steady, she found it and struck a match. Momentarily she saw the flare and her ghostly self reflected in the dark glass.

Having no experience of oil-lamps, she plumped for the easier option and lit the candle.

The flame flickered precariously as she forced herself to return to the landing. There were eight doors in all, but as luck would have it the first one she tried proved to be Saul's room.

She went in and glanced around, to find that, if anything, his bedroom was more spartan than her own.

A small pile of his personal belongings lay neatly on the chest of drawers, raising her hopes, only to dash them when no keys were among the loose change or beneath the folded handkerchief.

The light corduroy jacket he'd worn earlier was hanging over the back of a chair. Of course…that's where they would be.

Her heart beating fast, she put the candle carefully on the windowsill and, picking up the jacket, began to go through the various pockets.

'Looking for something?' The soft question tore a little shriek from her throat.

He was standing just beyond the range of the candlelight, a black and distinctly menacing figure in the surrounding gloom.

It was several seconds before she was able to speak. When she finally found her voice, even in her own ears it sounded high and frightened. 'I—I didn't hear you coming…' Then, more forcefully, 'You scared the living daylights out of me.'

'I would never have guessed.'

'How did you know where I was?'

His face was in deep shadow, but she fancied he smiled as he answered smoothly, 'By process of elimination.' Then, like a dagger-blow, 'So what are you looking for?'

Truth seemed the only option. 'The car keys.'

'For any particular reason?'

'You'd been gone a long time and I was getting anxious.'

'Really?'

Swallowing, she went on bravely, 'I thought you might have twisted your ankle or something…'

'How kind of you to be concerned.' The irony was more pronounced. 'But as you can see I'm quite unharmed…and I have a plan for revenge all worked out.'

As the words began to ricochet through her mind, deadly as flying bullets, he took off his sheepskin coat and, tossing it on to the bed, moved towards her.

Briefly the candlelight illuminated his hard, ruthless face. Standing transfixed, she saw he wasn't wearing his glasses and his eyes gleamed like silver.

All at once, as though a human breath had touched it, the candle-flame flickered and died.

CHAPTER THREE

HEART racing, the breath caught in her throat, she stood in the darkness while fear engulfed her, choking and lethal as acrid smoke.

When his hand touched her shoulder she made a small sound, a cross between a gasp and a moan, and began to tremble.

'Is something wrong?' he asked, with what sounded like mocking concern.

'Why did you do that?' She had a job to stop her teeth chattering.

'Do what?'

'Blow out the candle.'

'What makes you think I did it?'

'Well, I certainly didn't.'

In a reflective tone, he asked, 'Would a blind man be able to blow out a candle?'

Her voice ragged, she said, 'You tell me.'

'Yes, it's quite possible,' he admitted calmly. 'Just a matter of locating the heat source.'

'Then you did blow it out!'

'Why should I want to?'

'I don't know,' she cried wildly. 'A silly game, perhaps…?'

Sounding amused, he said, 'You mean like blind man's buff?'

The agitated words spilled out. 'I mean, to make us equal.'

'But it doesn't make us equal.' His voice became a purr. 'It gives me an advantage. Especially as you're afraid of the dark.'

She made an attempt to rally. 'Why are you so sure I'm afraid of the dark?'

'Aren't you?'

'Yes.' The admission was torn from her. Though she knew quite well it was foolish, she always had been.

'Then why don't we go downstairs?'

Relief filling her, she asked, 'Are there any matches in here?'

'Why do you need matches?'

'To light the candle.'

'You won't need a candle.' He found her hand and tucked it through his arm. 'I'll take you.'

Her relief drained away as he continued, with a kind of quiet menace, 'Come and experience, just for a minute or so, what it's like to be blind, to be led.'

Frightened afresh, wondering if the whole thing was some kind of macabre joke, she held back.

Feeling her resistance, he let her go.

There was no movement, no whisper of sound except her own breathing. The blackness was suffocating. After perhaps five seconds of pure panic, she cried, 'Saul, where are you?'

'I'm here.' He spoke softly, quite close to her ear.

With a half-stifled sob she turned towards the disembodied voice, and his arms closed around her. She looked up at him in the darkness and felt his breath against her cheek.

A moment later his mouth was covering hers. He kissed her lightly at first, then with a hungry passion that seared like flame and produced an answering blaze.

Shaken by a blinding wave of love, she clung to him until a sudden doubt, like a douche of icy water, doused the flame.

Why had he put his arms around her and kissed her? Maybe to reassure her? An impulse produced by their closeness? Or perhaps he'd guessed her real identity and was trying to make her give herself away?

Shuddering at the thought, she jerked free.

Coldly he asked, 'Just remembered I'm blind? Or did you kiss me back out of pity and then think better of kissing a blind man?'

Her voice shaking so much she could hardly speak, she managed, 'Your being blind has absolutely nothing to do with it. I—I just don't care to be touched or kissed by a— a virtual stranger.' Then, in desperation, 'Please…won't you take me down?'

'It will mean touching you,' he warned caustically.

'Oh, please…' she whispered.

Her legs were trembling but, as soon as his arm went about her waist, oddly convinced that he wouldn't let any harm come to her, she moved with relative confidence through the pitch-darkness.

'The stairs start here,' he cautioned, a moment or two later, 'and there are twelve steps.'

Like a child, she counted them aloud as they descended.

When they had crossed the hall, at the far end of the passageway she could see the welcome knife-edge of light under the kitchen door.

Beth, who was stretched at ease in front of the stove, lifted her handsome head to look at her master, then, satisfied she wasn't needed, laid it down again.

After the preceding darkness, the room seemed so bright that Autumn was momentarily dazzled. Blinking a little, she saw with a jolt that he was wearing his tinted glasses once more.

Or had she only imagined he'd discarded them? Imagined the silvery gleam of his eyes?

He released her hand, and grateful to be back once more

in the cheerful kitchen, she whispered, 'Thank you.' And meant it.

Just for an instant Saul looked uncomfortable, as though her thanks had disconcerted him, then, his face hardening, he turned away.

Going to the music centre, he slipped a cassette into the tape-deck, remarking casually over his shoulder, 'Something smells good.'

The last hour had been so fraught that Autumn had totally forgotten about the slices of baked ham and buttered potatoes she'd put in the oven.

Making an effort to push the doubts and fears to the back of her mind, she laid the table and made a green salad, while all the time her mouth remembered the feel of his, and the poignant, passionate theme of Rachmaninov's Second Piano Concerto—a favourite of Saul's which in the past she had often played—filled the room.

She never listened to it without the memories flooding back. Bitter-sweet memories that tightened round her heart like a giant fist, making her concentration falter and her capable hands fumble.

When at last everything was done, she told him, 'The meal's all ready.' She tried to sound carefree, unaffected. Without much success.

He waited politely until she was seated, then sat down opposite. After hesitating briefly, she filled two plates with food and set one in front of him.

Having thanked her, he ate deftly, without speaking, his expression remote as he listened to the beautiful music.

Watching his dark, shuttered face, Autumn wondered if it brought back memories for him.

Memories of those long-ago summer evenings at Cecilia Cottage. The casement windows thrown wide, the warm, sunny air carrying the scent of roses and honeysuckle into the low-beamed room. Herself at the piano. Saul lounging in a chintz-covered armchair, the coffee-percolator at his elbow. At ease, happy with each other's company...

Oblivious to the steady trickle of tears running down her cheeks, Autumn stared at him, loving him, finding the younger, carefree Saul beneath the lines which suffering and bitterness had etched on his handsome features.

When the music ended, memories retreating into the past, she wiped away the tears with her hands and tried to gather herself to cope with the present.

His peat-dark head tilted a little to one side, Saul appeared to be looking straight at her once more, and she saw, with a hollow emptiness in the pit of her stomach, that his hard, strong-boned face seemed full of sardonic satisfaction.

She was almost ready, but not quite, when he queried, 'You find that piece very moving?'

Knowing it was useless to deny it, Autumn swallowed and answered, 'I've always loved Rachmaninov.' She was aware that her voice was unsteady.

Seeing he'd put down his knife and fork, and afraid of any more searching questions, she forced herself to ask, 'Would you like cheese and biscuits?'

'Just coffee, please. But first finish your own meal.'

Wondering how he knew her plate was barely touched, she said jerkily, 'I've had as much as I want.'

As soon as she rose, he left his own seat and, having opened the glass doors of the stove, settled himself in an armchair facing her, Beth at his feet.

With the uncomfortable sensation that from behind his tinted glasses he was watching her every move, Autumn washed the few dishes and made a pot of coffee.

Ever since their return to the living-room she had, on one level of consciousness, been trying to convince herself that her panic had been only a lot of fear and trembling over nothing.

But the words he'd spoken just before the candle went out began once more to whirl around in her mind, bumping and banging against her self-possession.

Knowing how easily he seemed to pick up what she was thinking and feeling, she strove to smother her disquiet as she set the tray of coffee down on the small oblong table between the armchairs.

Filling two cups with the fragrant brew, she handed Saul's to him with care.

'Thank you.' Having sipped, he remarked, 'Clever of you to know I like my after-dinner coffee black and sugar-less…'

His words broke into her introspection, jolting her. Taking a deep breath, she said levelly, 'Cleverness doesn't come into it. You told me you didn't like to be fussed over.'

He made the gesture of a fencer acknowledging a successful riposte. Then he said blandly, 'So you expected me to help myself to sugar and milk?'

About to say yes, Autumn realised she'd put neither on the tray. And somehow he knew.

When he suddenly got up, tall and dark and dangerous, she stiffened. But he merely rattled the poker around to establish how low the fire was, before throwing a couple of big logs into the stove.

After pausing for a moment by the music centre, he returned to his chair without putting on another tape, and the silence, full of uneasy fears and growing tension, soon became nerve-racking.

When Autumn could bear it no longer, she blurted out the question that was busy spawning chimeras. 'Earlier you said you had a plan for revenge all worked out…' She licked her dry lips. 'What did you mean?'

He appeared to look straight at her, and his mouth twisted in a strange little smile as he asked, 'What did you think I meant?'

'I—I'd no idea.'

His smile deepening, he told her, 'I was referring to my latest book. I usually think out my plots while I'm walking… Have you by any chance read *The Lightning Tree*?'

She had. But not by chance. She'd bought it because it was Saul's and, reading it, she had shrivelled inside.

Trying to look at things objectively, she had told herself that he had *needed* to write it out, to get rid of all the anger and bitterness.

It had certainly been full of both.

Strangely loath to admit she had read that powerful and emotive tale, Autumn brushed back her silky half-fringe with an agitated hand, and lied jerkily, 'No… No, I haven't.'

His face bleak as the moors outside, he told her, 'It's the story of Sean Calder, a nineteenth-century politician, and Anna Maune, a girl ten years younger than himself, who imagined she was in love with him.

'She wrecked both his impending marriage and his career, then disappeared from his life after an accident left him crippled…'

The initials of the characters were the same as hers and Saul's, and the similarity between the hero's fate and Saul's own was much too strong to be coincidental. The main difference was that Saul's marriage had gone ahead, and he'd managed to find a new career.

'I needed you here because I'm about to start work on the sequel.' An icy purpose in his voice, he added, '*The Tamarind Tree* is going to be the tale of Sean's revenge.'

The words could have been quite innocuous, yet somehow they'd held a silky threat, and Autumn felt a shudder run down her spine.

From being apprehensive about the coming weeks, she was now positively scared.

Loving him so, longing to be with him, wanting to take

care of him in some small way, she had accepted the risks, hoping against hope that everything would be all right, that they could work quietly together, form some kind of platonic, healing relationship.

But loving him, wanting to take care of him, she now realised, was about as safe as loving and wanting to take care of a wounded tiger.

She might have made a bad mistake coming to this isolated spot with a man who still felt so bitter about the past. A man who clearly believed in revenge.

If he discovered her true identity she could get emotionally mauled.

And he would enjoy watching her bleed.

That was the most terrifying thought of all.

But if she allowed it to throw her, she might give herself away. Somehow, though it wouldn't be easy, she had to keep her self-control and play it cool...

Becoming aware of the taut silence, she looked up and saw that once again he appeared to be staring straight at her.

Taking a deep breath, she forced herself into speech. 'How do you plan your work, Mr Cresswell?'

'Why so formal?' He smiled wolfishly. 'Earlier, when you were afraid of the dark, you called me Saul.'

The room whirled hideously around her head. 'I—I'm sorry... I...'

'Don't apologise. I was about to suggest we dispense with formality.' Relief made her feel weak as he added, 'Perhaps I could call you Elizabeth?'

Before she could pull herself together enough to make any answer, he went on smoothly, 'But you were asking how I plan my work... In the initial stages I walk a lot. I think better on the move. Only when I've got the characters and the structure of the plot clear in my mind do I start to actually write.

'Sometimes, if a particularly strong emotional theme takes over, the plot alters and I find I've a different ending. But, with this story, the revenge element is so powerful that the ending is unlikely to change.'

Knowing only too well what the answer would be, Autumn was still impelled to ask, 'How *does* it end?'

His mouth twisting into a thin, cruel smile that made her shiver, he said, 'You'll have to wait and see.'

Needing time to recover some degree of composure, she suggested jerkily, 'Shall I make another pot of coffee?'

'How did you know I'm a coffee addict?'

In contrast with his previous grimness, the question sounded light, almost teasing.

Trying for the same light tone, she answered, 'I'm quite good at guessing.'

As she picked up the tray and headed for the kitchen area he observed, 'I'm not bad myself.' Deliberately turning it into a kind of game, he added, 'And my guess is you have no shoes on.'

She froze in her tracks, wanting to deny he was right but unable to. 'I—I just slipped them off to warm my feet.'

His voice velvet-soft, he remarked, 'I used to know a girl who never wore shoes if she could help it. She was like some barefoot woodland nymph, with long russet-coloured chair and slanting green-gold eyes...'

Struggling to keep the shock out of her voice, Autumn said prosaically, 'If your nymph had lived here she'd have worn shoes. These stone flags are cold!'

While she refilled the coffee-pot she called herself all kinds of a fool. Discarding her shoes had been a bad mistake, but momentarily she'd forgotten just how acute his hearing was.

'So we're even on the guessing,' he remarked as she returned to the fire.

Needing to say something, she objected, 'Yours was hardly a *guess*.'

He shrugged. 'Losing one's sight has some compensations.' Then, with a tinge of bitterness, 'Don't you want to know how it happened? People are usually curious.'

Clenching her jaw, she fought back tears while she concentrated on pouring the coffee. Then, taking her seat again, she managed to say levelly, 'I read in *Top People* that it had been in a car crash.'

'It was a head-on collision. The driver of the other vehicle was gaoled for a year. He was blamed for the accident because he had a very high blood-alcohol level. But it wasn't solely his fault... I wasn't over the limit, but I was in a blind rage.' Flatly, he added, 'If I'd been driving with my usual concentration I might have managed to avoid him.'

She leaned forward to insist, 'But you can't be sure of that... And you can't blame yourself...'

'Then, who can I blame? The woman who made me so angry that I should never have been behind the wheel?' He spoke with such chilling ferocity that she shrank back.

A weight of cold lead in place of her heart, she said, barely above a whisper, 'It seems to me that's where the blame rightly belongs.'

'I wonder.'

He swallowed his coffee and replaced the cup before rising to his feet.

Suddenly, before she could guess his intention, he was standing over her, stooping a little, his hand resting lightly on her throat.

Feeling her swallow convulsively, he said with cool arrogance, 'The description you gave of yourself was much too vague. I find I don't really like talking to some faceless person.'

'Oh, but I...'

'Just steel yourself for a moment.'

Unable to fight such sardonic determination, she sat rigid, the hairs on the back of her neck rising as his hands moved to cup her face lightly and discover the delicate bones and smooth skin.

Four years ago her teenage complexion hadn't been quite so flawless, and puppy-fat had slightly blurred the purity of her fine bone-structure.

Praying his touch would reveal only today's woman, not yesterday's adolescent, she held her breath while his fingertips smoothed the silky curve of her brows, closed her eyelids, and followed the high cheekbones to the clean lines of her jaw.

After a tantalising pause, they returned to trace her small, neat nose and short upper lip, before going on to explore the generous curve of her mouth which, despite all her efforts, trembled beneath his touch.

When his index finger parted her lips to rub across the pearly evenness of her teeth, unable to stand any more, she jerked back with a half-stifled protest that was almost a sob.

He was apparently satisfied; his hands dropped away and he resumed his own seat without comment.

After a moment, he commanded idly, 'Tell me about yourself.'

'There's not much to tell.' In spite of all her efforts her voice sounded hoarse and strained.

'You mentioned a fiancé. What was his name?'

'Richard Mallard.'

'What did he do?'

'Richard was a computer expert.'

'Why did your engagement break up?'

'We just weren't suited,' she said lamely.

'Did you sleep together?'

She was startled into answering sharply, 'I don't think that's any of your business.'

He lifted his shoulders in a slight shrug. 'I just wondered. Most engaged couples seem to these days.'

When she said nothing, he asked with a touch of derision, 'Don't tell me he didn't want to?'

Oh, yes, he'd wanted to.

In an attempt to put the past behind her, and establish a real relationship, she'd agreed to Richard's demand that they should become lovers. But after he'd arranged a cosy weekend in the Catskills, she'd found herself unable to go through with it.

Frustrated and furious, he had dropped his charming mask and, after showing her a not so pleasant side to his character, had stormed out of the hotel, leaving her shamed and humiliated.

When, unwilling to talk about Richard and what she still saw as her failure as a woman, Autumn remained silent, Saul asked with unnerving perception, 'Are you afraid of close physical contact?'

'Why should I be afraid?' she said defensively.

'More than once you've told me you don't like to be touched. After I kissed you I felt you shudder, and a minute ago, while I was touching your face, you were so nervous I thought you were going to faint...'

As though to demonstrate, he reached out and trailed a fingertip down her cheek, making her jump violently.

With a glint of triumph, he asked, 'Does everyone's touch affect you so strongly, or is it just mine?'

Summoning up every ounce of will-power she possessed, Autumn said obliquely, 'I like to have my own personal space... But I thought that was one of the reasons you gave me the job.'

'So it was.' As she watched the creases beside his mouth deepen in a smile, attractive as it was mirthless, he attacked from a different angle. 'I take it you were an only child?'

'Yes,' she answered reluctantly.

With a suddenness that took her by surprise, he queried, 'Where did you say you were brought up?'

Her mind a complete blank, her mouth a little open, she gaped at him stupidly.

He raised a dark brow. 'Elmgreen, was it…?'

'Yes… Yes, that's right.' She grasped at the lifeline.

Smoothly, he queried, 'Are you planning to go back to Elmgreen when this job is over?'

'I… No, I don't think so.'

'Have you friends and relatives still living there?'

'No.'

'You must have spent a somewhat solitary childhood?' When she failed to respond to that remark, he said, with no change of tone, 'Perhaps I should get out the thumb-screws.'

She caught her breath. 'Wh-what do you mean?'

'I mean this is more like an inquisition than a conversation.'

'I'm sorry…I—I'm rather tired. It must be the journey.' She seized on the first excuse that came to mind, adding desperately, 'I was hoping to have an early night.'

As she spoke, the wall-clock chimed the half-hour.

'Dear me,' he murmured with mild derision, 'and it's nine-thirty already.'

He rose to his feet and, leaving the kitchen door wide so that it spilt light into the passage, led her to the small table in the hall. Removing the glass chimney from the oil-lamp, he proceeded to light the wick with a deft competence that made it difficult to believe he couldn't actually see.

Replacing the glass, he offered politely, 'Allow me to light you upstairs.'

He led the way, his shadow leaping menacingly ahead, black on white walls.

As soon as they reached the broad landing he handed her

the oil-lamp. 'Sleep well, Elizabeth. When you turn out the light, don't let the darkness frighten you.'

Reacting to the edge of mockery in his low, attractive voice, she said steadily, 'I won't.'

Turning to go back down, he added over his shoulder, 'And don't forget, you won't be really alone. I'll be quite close.'

Something about that soft rider made her skin goose-pimple.

Trying to ignore the frisson of fear, she went into the bathroom and, having put the oil-lamp down on the wide windowsill, washed her face and hands and cleaned her teeth.

As she crossed the landing to her room, she could faintly hear another Rachmaninov piano concerto being played.

Disturbing thoughts darting about her head like minnows in a muddy pond, she undressed and climbed into the high, old-fashioned bed.

It was cold. Her breath made a white mist on the air, and the bed felt like an icy waste. She wished her nightie was long enough to wrap her feet in.

Hating the idea of the waiting darkness closing in on her, she had to make a positive effort before she could bring herself to stretch out a hand and extinguish the lamp.

That done, she pulled the thick duvet up to her chin and, closing her eyes tightly, lay shivering. But not for long. The combination of old-fashioned feather-bed and modern duvet worked well, and in a matter of minutes she was comfortably warm.

Physically and emotionally worn out after such a fraught day, she was gradually relaxing, slipping into sleep, when a thought surfaced that jolted her into wakefulness.

Earlier that evening when, taken by surprise, she had failed to answer Saul's query about where she'd been brought up, he'd suggested Elmgreen...and she'd agreed.

But when he'd asked her during the interview, she had told him Oakgreen.

Had naming the wrong village been an innocent mistake on his part? Or had she fallen into a carefully laid trap?

No, surely not. Heart thudding against her ribs, she tried to reassure herself. If she had, wouldn't he have pounced?

Unless he *knew* who she was, and was playing some deep, cruel game.

Hampered by her own guilty knowledge, it was difficult to assess how many pieces of the jigsaw he might have recognised and put together, and how much was simply in her mind.

Four years was a long time. But he certainly hadn't forgotten Autumn Milski. Neither had he forgiven her.

Though surely his recollection of the eighteen-year-old Autumn would be quite different from the woman he knew as Elizabeth Shandon?

But if by any chance it wasn't, and he suspected the truth, why hadn't he challenged her? Maybe he *was* playing with her as a cat played with a mouse…

Her uneasy thoughts having come full circle, they continued to spin round and round in her head, making sleep impossible. But though she lay wide awake for what seemed an age, she didn't hear Saul come to bed.

It must have been early in the morning before she finally fell asleep and, when she did, her slumbers were restless, haunted by a series of dreams. Dreams which always started with Saul close and loving, but invariably ended with him ignoring her pleas and walking away from her without a backward glance.

Daybreak came as a blessed relief.

Lying in bed, she watched a rack of clouds scudding along, and some black birds being blown about like pieces of litter in the windy sky. Gradually, without her being aware of it, her eyelids drooped and she drifted off to sleep again.

It was well after ten o'clock before, heavy-eyed and still unrefreshed, she struggled out of bed and shivered her way to the bathroom.

After a shower, which rather to her surprise proved to be good and hot and trouble-free, she began to feel a great deal better, and her spirits rose.

The house seemed altogether more friendly, and in the light of day a lot of the previous night's fears appeared foolish.

Dressed in a calf-length skirt of soft warm wool and a sweater that echoed the green of her eyes, she decided on socks, rather than tights, and flat shoes. Her long hair brushed into a smooth fall of russet silk that curled under a little at the ends, she made her way downstairs to the cheerful kitchen.

Beth, who was lying on the mat in front of the blazing stove, got up and came over, plume of a tail gently waving.

Pleased with this sign of acceptance, Autumn stooped to stroke the handsome head, before looking up to find Saul sitting at his desk, apparently deep in thought, the tape recorder in front of him.

He was wearing a black polo-necked sweater and his dark hair was a little rumpled, as though he'd run his fingers through it. Control, rather than serenity, sculpted the planes and angles of his face.

His eyes were invisible behind the tinted lenses, but his firm yet sensitive mouth had a masculine beauty that always made her yearn to touch it with her own.

In spite of everything, her heart lifted at the sight of him. 'Good morning.' Her voice was tinged with the gladness she felt.

'Good morning. You sound cheerful. Does that mean you slept well?'

'Very well, thank you,' she lied. Then she asked, 'Can I get you something to eat?'

'I had breakfast hours ago,' he said wryly.

His sheepskin coat hanging behind the door suggested that he'd also been out with the dog.

A glance at the clock confirming that the time was approaching eleven, she said, 'I'm sorry I'm so late. I'll make sure I'm earlier tomorrow.'

'Until I actually want to start work, there's no need. I'm quite capable of getting my own toast and coffee.' His words sounded cool, dismissive.

A moment later he was speaking quietly into the tape recorder once more, sketching in an outline of the first chapter.

Flattened, she retreated to the kitchen area and helped herself to orange juice and a bowl of cornflakes.

Accustomed to browsing through a morning paper, she used as a substitute a tattered paperback cookery-book entitled *Everyday Cooking Made Easy*.

Leafing idly through its well-thumbed pages, she recalled the remark Saul had made about George's culinary skills, and smiled.

Saul had once been no mean cook and sometimes, at Cecilia Cottage, he had taken a turn at making a tasty pasta dish for supper...

'About finished?'

The object of her thoughts had left his desk so quietly that he was at her elbow before she realised he'd moved.

'Yes.' She put down her spoon.

'Then if you're ready I'll show you around the rest of the house before I take my morning walk.'

In spite of the polite phrasing it was undoubtedly an order.

She glanced up quickly, trying to read his expression, but behind the dark glasses his face was inscrutable.

Wondering why he hadn't just left her to look round on her own, she got up obediently and followed him.

The white-walled, black-beamed manor-cum-farm-house was a rambling old place, with many nooks and crannies and passages, and a back staircase, but Saul clearly knew every inch of it and led the way with a quiet confidence.

'This long room is the original farm kitchen,' he told her, 'with a separate pantry at the end. The pump on the sink is still connected with the covered well which provides our water-supply.'

Noticing that the steady hum she now accepted as a background noise sounded much closer, Autumn asked, 'Where is the generator housed?'

'Beyond that door—' he pointed '—in what used to be the scullery.'

Turning his back on the kitchen quarters, he conducted her down a wide, flagged passage towards the front of the house. 'But what I really want you to see is through here.'

Some subtle change in his tone alerted her. The small hairs on the back of her neck rose, and a chill that had nothing to do with the cold ran up and down her spine, making her shiver.

CHAPTER FOUR

AUTUMN glanced apprehensively at him, but his dark face was bland, unrevealing, as he opened the first door.

Though he appeared to want to show her nothing more sinister than the two main rooms, the pricking in her thumbs persisted.

'This used to be the living-room.'

A large room, it had a wide stone fireplace and a flagged floor, and was obviously unused, the air chilly, the old-fashioned furnishings dusty and cobwebby.

Throwing the last door wide, Saul put a hand at her waist, urging her forward. 'And this is the parlour.'

The parlour, a beautiful room with an inglenook fireplace and wide oak floorboards, was empty except for a huge sheepskin rug lying in front of the hearth, a couple of black leather armchairs, a low table and, standing to one side of the latticed windows, a baby grand piano.

Hanging on the wall beyond the piano was a head-and-shoulders portrait of a girl Autumn immediately recognised as herself.

If it had been a torture-chamber she couldn't have been more horrified. With a gasp she recoiled, stumbling into the man behind her, dislodging his glasses.

His hands encircling her upper arms, he held her against his muscular chest, while she tried to regain both her mental and physical balance.

'You seem startled?' he remarked, with the same mocking concern he'd evinced when the candle went out.

'I—I'm sorry,' she stammered, instinctively making an effort to hide just how shocked she was. 'It—it was just so unexpected... The piano, I mean.'

After a second or two, she regained her balance and tried to move away, but his grip tightened painfully, as though he had no intention of letting her go.

Panic had stopped her breath, when his fingers slackened their hold, releasing her.

She took a couple of shaky steps before turning to make her escape. Tall and dark, he was filling the doorway. Shock hit her anew as she looked directly into his eyes.

'Your eyes...' Her voice was barely above a whisper as she spoke her thoughts aloud. 'They don't look... I mean there's no obvious sign of them being injured.'

'Are you saying I should be thankful for small mercies?'

She cringed at the bitterness in his voice. 'No, I wasn't saying that.'

But, staring into those silvery eyes, she was fiercely glad that their beauty was unmarred.

'Only I wondered what... Why...?' Her voice tailed off.

Tearing her gaze away with an effort, she stooped to pick up his lightweight glasses, which had fallen on to the polished black floorboards, and handed them to him.

'I received a heavy blow to the temple and the optic nerve was damaged,' he told her curtly as he put the glasses back on.

She found herself wondering why he wore them. Though in some ways she preferred him to. It was unnerving to look into his eyes when they looked straight back at her, and appeared to *see* her.

He turned to go and, only too eager to escape from that disturbing room, she followed him back to the kitchen on legs that shook like jelly.

As soon as he lifted the sheepskin jacket from its hook, Beth was by his side, alert and waiting.

Striving to act normally, to hide the fact that she was still so shaken, Autumn queried, 'What time will you be back?'

'Probably late afternoon if I take the track over to Moorend.'

'Oh... But it's almost lunchtime...'

His hand on the latch, he said, 'I often don't bother with lunch when I'm working.'

Wanting, despite everything, to say, Take care, she somehow bit back the anxious words.

Casually he added, 'Make yourself at home while I'm gone. Try out your piano...'

A moment later the door closed behind him.

For a second or two she was rooted to the spot, unable to move, then, heart pounding, she stumbled to the window.

Outside it looked bleak and threatening, the sky pewter-grey and heavy with cloud. A few fine flakes of snow were swirling down.

Bareheaded, the collar of his jacket turned up, Saul was following a track that headed deeper into the dark moors, the dog close by his side.

Feeling sick and her stomach churning, she watched until he was out of sight, before turning away and sinking into the nearest chair.

'Try out your piano...' His last words seemed branded into her brain with letters of fire.

Her girlhood dream, which she'd once confessed to Saul, had been to have her own baby grand. On her fifteenth birthday he'd bought her a small but perfect replica—she had it still—and had promised quizzically, 'One day I'll buy you a real one.'

It had been obvious from the start that he was showing her the parlour for a reason.

So why, after making it clear that he knew her true identity, had he just walked out? Why continue this charade?

The unpalatable answer was that it was all part of some plan. Part of his revenge.

But it didn't make sense. She had been settled in the States for almost four years, so how could he have known that she was coming back to England?

She hadn't decided until about six weeks ago when, only a short while after the break-up of her engagement, her apologetic employer had told her that his new wife was to be his secretary, and she'd found herself out of a job.

Notice to quit her furnished apartment had been the last straw. On appealing, she had been told that the old brownstone in which she'd lived for the past three years had been sold, and the new owner wanted it empty to refurbish it.

But Saul couldn't possibly have known that circumstances would drive her home, nor could he have known she would see a copy of *Top People*, let alone apply for the position advertised.

So to all intents and purposes it was impossible that he could have planned any of this.

Yet she knew he had.

And, given that knowledge, everything fitted in, including the frightening little scene in his bedroom, when he'd said with quiet menace, 'Come and experience, just for a minute or so, what it's like to be blind, to be led.' With hindsight she now felt certain it had been as deliberate as showing her the parlour.

So what would be his next move? Was he planning to keep applying different kinds of pressure until she finally cracked?

She shuddered, and shuddered again.

While she was sure he wouldn't hurt her physically, she knew she had to get away.

Once clear of the moors, she could phone Mr Baber's office and make certain George or someone was sent up to Farthing Beck immediately.

And surely they could get in touch with one of the people who had already been interviewed for the job of secretary? Unwilling to add to her guilt, she didn't want his work to be held up for any length of time.

But it was imperative that she should go *now*, before his return.

Jumping to her feet, she made an effort to stay calm and focus her mind. The first thing she must do was find the car keys.

On trembling legs she hastened upstairs and forced herself to go into his room. Showing how close she was to panic, she found herself glancing continually at the door, wondering if he might be creeping up on her as he had done the previous night.

She searched swiftly, but thoroughly, first in his pockets and then through the chest of drawers, all the time trying to ignore the unpleasant thought that he would almost certainly have taken them with him to foil any such bid on her part.

Clenching her teeth, she decided that if the worst came to the worst and she couldn't find them, even if it meant leaving everything behind, she'd go on foot to the village and beg help there.

Anything was better than staying at Farthing Beck to endure Saul's subtle yet sadistic revenge.

Her last hope gone, she was about to fetch her coat and make a run for it, when suddenly she saw the bunch of keys lying on the bedside table in full view.

It wasn't like Saul to make such a bad mistake, but 'sometimes even excellent Homer nods'.

Her heart beating a mad tattoo, she grabbed them and, running into her own room, bundled her clothes back into the suitcase with frantic haste.

Having pulled on her coat and gathered up her belongings, the case bumping against her legs, she hurried down the stairs.

She was nearing the bottom when her foot slipped from the step. Thrown off-balance, she stumbled and fell awkwardly, her right ankle buckling beneath her.

Struggling to her feet, she put her weight on it and yelped. But, driven by fear, she somehow picked up her things, and despite the pain headed for the door.

As she opened it white flakes swirled round her like confetti, and she saw that snow was beginning to fall in earnest now from a louring sky.

Anxious about Saul, she frowned at the worsening weather. When she reached Feldon she would ask the people at the Green Man to check that he'd got home safely, she decided, as, the ignition keys in her hand, she turned towards the car.

Mouth hanging foolishly open, she stared at the empty space, now scoured by wind-blown snow, where the Rover had been standing.

This had to be some trick of Saul's. Knowing the car was no longer there, he must have deliberately left the keys for her to find. A kind of torture by hope.

But *where* had it gone? *How* had it gone?

Shudder after shudder running through her, she pushed her luggage back inside and, with just her bag over her shoulder, headed for the bridge, gritting her teeth against the pain.

She'd gone only a few yards when her injured ankle gave way under her and she went sprawling, knocking all the breath from her body and bruising herself on the cobbles.

Struggling up, she was forced to admit that there was no way she would even make it to the other side of the bridge, let alone to the village.

It seemed that fate was on Saul's side.

In spite of the bitter wind and swirling snow, she was

sweating with pain by the time she'd hobbled back to the house and pulled off her coat.

For a while she huddled by the stove, then, gripped by a compelling need, a kind of compulsion, she left the cheerful living-room and made her painful way along the passage to the parlour.

Even though she knew what to expect, it still came as a shock, making her stomach turn over. Steeling herself, she drew a deep breath and stared at the picture hanging above the piano.

Looking back gravely was a young girl with shining russet hair tumbling round her shoulders, a creamy skin, slanting green-gold eyes, and a passionate mouth.

The face had a fascinating, haunting quality, as though the artist himself had been bewitched, held in thrall by that poignant beauty.

Was that how Saul had seen her all those years ago?

No, surely not. If he had, he would have loved her.

And he hadn't loved her.

Foolishly she had thought he had. Had fondly imagined he was waiting until she was old enough to tell her how he felt and ask her to marry him.

It wasn't that she'd had any confidence in her own attraction. It was simply that she had known with a quiet certainty that, body and soul, they would always belong to one another. And, loving him as she did, it hadn't seemed possible he could remain untouched by such a wealth of emotion.

An emotion she'd only been able to express in her music.

Taking her eyes from that somehow disturbing picture, she hobbled over to the piano which stood near to the casement windows.

In the deep windowsill was another tall-chimneyed oil-lamp, and beside it a short piece of loosely woven white cord and a small pair of scissors, as though someone had recently renewed the wick.

Looking through the diamond-leaded panes, she saw with anxiety that the snow was falling even faster now, drifting against the stone sills and weighing down the green arms of the pine.

Surely Saul wouldn't go on in this? Please God, she prayed silently, don't let any harm come to him.

The baby grand was an old and very beautiful instrument. Autumn could see herself reflected in its patina. Sitting down on the stool, she opened the lid almost reverently and ran her hands lightly over the keys.

It was months since she'd played. Her fingers felt stiff, out of practice, and because of her injured ankle she was unable to use the pedals properly. But the tone was wonderfully mellow, the ivory keys like silk beneath her touch, and within minutes her fingers had recaptured all their former skill and magic.

Caught up in the spell she was weaving, she forgot about everything but the music flowing from her fingertips. Instinctively she had begun with one of Saul's favourites, the love theme from Tchaikovsky's *Romeo and Juliet*...

When her parents had moved into Cecilia Cottage she had been a quiet, shy girl of thirteen. The same age as Juliet. And, like Juliet, she had fallen in love at first sight. Deeply. Passionately. Irrevocably.

Saul had lived in The Rowans, the single-storey creeper-covered house next door. Having inherited a blazing talent as well as a comfortable sum of money from his maternal grandfather, Sir Giles Waring, at the age of twenty-two he had already started to make a name for himself as an artist.

Her mother and father were out almost every evening. His socially active, well-to-do parents had died together in a plane crash the previous summer.

Perhaps, knowing what it was like to be lonely, he had

recognised the symptoms in Autumn, and somehow, in spite of the age-gap, and the difference in their backgrounds, they had become friends.

A lover of music, he had encouraged her playing, accompanying her to music festivals and listening for hours while she practised.

Her parents had hoped she would become a concert pianist, but, recognising her own limitations, she had accepted the fact that she would never be first-rate, and been glad.

Though contented enough in its way, her life had always been a lonely one because of her parents' commitment to music. Knowing from first-hand experience how demanding such a career was, she hadn't wanted to mortgage her whole future.

Rather, she'd dreamt of spending it with Saul, of loving him and being loved in return, of making a full and happy family life for their children.

A simple enough dream. Only it had never come true. It had been shattered for good on her eighteenth birthday.

From the first he had treated her like a younger sister. Except that none of Autumn's school-friends had such a close, harmonious relationship with their brothers.

He'd advised, protected, encouraged, and helped to broaden her mind, adding modern history, archaeology, and art to her other interests.

With his superior knowledge of life, he'd taught the shy, gauche girl the social graces, providing her with poise and an outward air of confidence. But, most precious of all, he'd unstintingly given her his time and companionship.

The only thing still to come—when she was old enough—had been his declaration of love.

Though, over the years, Saul had never been short of girlfriends, they had all seemed casual, unimportant, posing no threat to the special relationship Autumn and he shared.

Or to the future she'd envisaged.

In itself the age difference had meant nothing to her, but when she'd grasped that from a conventional point of view it wasn't socially acceptable for a man of twenty-six to love a schoolgirl, she'd begged to be allowed to leave the all-girls' school at seventeen.

Seeing no good reason for such a move, her parents had insisted on her staying for her final year.

A year which, to Autumn, impatient for it to end, had seemed all too long.

One lovely June evening, having no current girlfriend, Saul had invited her to a party being thrown by one of his married friends. Thrilled and excited by what she had regarded as her first real date, she had fantasised about what might happen when he took her home.

From time to time he had given her a brotherly hug or a chaste kiss on the cheek. But, though innocent and untouched to the point of being naïve, over the past weeks she had noticed a change in his attitude towards her, a tension that instinct told her was sexual.

Now she was nearly eighteen he might be seeing her as a woman and treating her like one instead of like a schoolgirl. She shivered with excitement at the thought.

The party was in full swing when they arrived, and Autumn felt artlessly elated to realise she was with by far the most attractive man there.

She wasn't the only one to realise it.

Joanna, a stunning blonde, introduced by their host as a photographic model, was glamorous and sophisticated, seductive and experienced, and from the same class of society as Saul.

Everything Autumn was not.

Ignoring the younger girl completely, Joanna made a dead set at him.

Though it was carefully hidden, Autumn sensed his re-

sponse to the blatant sexual invitation and felt embarrassed
and awkward and bitterly jealous.

Her evening ruined, she was only too happy to fall in
with Saul's suggestion that they leave early.

She wasn't so happy when, having seen her safely home,
he refused to come in, and left her with just a casual, 'Sleep
well.'

Standing at the window, watching him drive away down
the tree-lined road, she knew with bleak certainty where he
was going and why.

From then on, though Saul refused to discuss the new
woman in his life, Autumn knew he was seeing Joanna.
Eaten up with jealousy, she could no longer relax and be
happy, and their old, comfortable relationship was spoilt.

But no matter how serious it was on Saul's side, Autumn
felt convinced that on the blonde's it was merely sexual
attraction rather than love.

Lucy, one of Autumn's class-mates, unwittingly encouraged this view one day. Displaying a glossy magazine with
the model's beautifully made-up face on the cover, she said
importantly, 'Her name's Joanna; she's Sir William James's
daughter. She's friends with Stephy, my eldest sister. They
were at art school together... She has a red Porsche and
lives in one of those posh new flats facing the war me-
morial...'

When Autumn sat silent and frozen, Lucy went on,
'Hasn't she got it all? Wish I could be so lucky. The only
thing I wouldn't like is the constant dieting. Still, it must
be worth it. She only has to beckon to get any man she
fancies... According to the papers, she's had a string of
affairs, but she soon gets tired of her lovers... She told
Stephy she's only having fun until she can find herself a
rich husband...'

Though in one way it was what she wanted to hear, for

Saul's sake Autumn felt angry and resentful that Joanna was just amusing herself with him.

That evening he came round. Sensing the still-smouldering anger, he asked, 'What's wrong, Autumn?'

'Nothing's wrong,' she mumbled, refusing to meet his eyes.

Lifting her chin, making her look at him, he said, 'You haven't seemed yourself for weeks now. Come on, out with it. What are you brooding about?'

'It's *her*...'

For a moment he looked surprised. Then, a hardness creeping into his voice, he said, 'You mean Joanna? What about her?'

The words poured out, full of bitterness and jealousy. 'Don't imagine she cares twopence for you; she doesn't... You're only one of a string of lovers...'

'What do you know about such things? You're still a child.'

That remark burnt into her soul like acid. If only he'd thought of her as a woman rather than a child, he might never have got involved with Joanna.

'I'm not a child!' she denied shrilly. 'And I've been told how she flits from one man to another.'

'Whatever she does, it's no business of yours.'

He'd never used that tone to her before, and tears filled her eyes.

Hurting, she lashed out at him. 'You're being a fool! She's just amusing herself with you while she finds herself a rich husband.'

Quietly he said, 'Maybe she's found one.' And just as quietly walked out.

Saul's parting shot still echoing in her mind, Autumn cried herself to sleep that night, cried as though her heart would break.

Of course he hadn't meant it, she reassured herself. He'd

only said it because he was angry with her. Still, it was the
first time they had ever seriously quarrelled, and it tore her
apart.

Next morning, seeing her blotched face and swollen eyes
in the bathroom mirror, Autumn was glad her parents were
away on tour with the Academy Orchestra.

They had been sorry to leave her alone, with her birthday
coming up, but it was the last tour they would make before
moving to New York, where Daniel Milski was due to take
up the post of resident conductor to the New World
Symphony Orchestra.

Pointing out that they were giving up their rented cottage, they had tried to persuade her to travel to the States
with them.

She had said she would sooner find a job and a bed-sit
locally; she didn't fancy living in America. The real reason
was that she couldn't bring herself to leave Saul.

Saul, who always had been, and still was, her reason for
living.

Sick at heart, she knew that when he came round she
would need to hide her real feelings and apologise.

Her apology ready, she spent the next two days on ten-
terhooks, waiting for him.

He didn't come.

The following evening, with the excuse of returning a
borrowed book, she called in on Lucy. A casual question
brought the information that Joanna was away. Autumn
sighed. So that couldn't have been the reason Saul hadn't
appeared.

When Thursday came, with still no sign of him, she
faced the fact that he wasn't going to come. Unable to bear
the thought of losing his friendship entirely, she braced
herself and went round to The Rowans.

The long room on the north side of the one-storey house

had been converted into a studio, and she guessed he would be in there painting.

Normally she wouldn't have dreamt of interrupting him while he was working, but now she was in such a state that she no longer cared.

When she appeared at the open French windows he looked up, surprised, and, judging by his frown, not over-pleased to see her.

'I—I'm sorry to disturb you but I wanted to apologise.' Flushed and close to tears, she went on, scarcely above a whisper, 'I shouldn't have said what I did about Joanna...'

His dark face softened.

'Please say you forgive me,' she begged.

'I forgive you.'

'No, seriously.'

His lips twitched. 'Seriously, I forgive you.'

He was taking it far too lightly. While she had been torn apart, he seemed intent on teasing.

Overwrought, her face crumpling as though she was the child he'd called her, she turned to run. In a flash he was there, encircling her wrist, stopping her.

When she tried to jerk free he pulled her into his arms and held her close. 'Don't be foolish, Autumn. Of course I forgive you.'

After a moment he set her away a little, and, taking her face between his hands, with a kind of impatient tenderness used his thumbs to wipe away the tears. 'To prove it I'll take you out to dinner on Friday.'

Friday, the last day in September, was her eighteenth birthday. Joy filled her that he had remembered.

He gave her behind a playful slap. 'Now get along and let me finish this commission.' As she turned to hurry away, he added, 'I'll pick you up at seven.'

The following day she drew some of her savings and bought herself glamorous new undies, and an expensive boutique dress—a sophisticated greeny-gold silk-lined chiffon, with a softly draped bodice cut daringly low and a skirt that swirled around her slender legs.

Determined to leave the schoolgirl image behind, she went to the hairdresser and had her long hair cut and brightened so that it hugged her skull like a cap of burnished bronze feathers, emphasising her superb bone-structure and making her eyes seem enormous.

Her head feeling oddly light, she made her way to the beauty salon and emerged with a professional make-up, her brows tidied and shaped and her long lashes darkened.

Officially a woman now, she fully intended to look like one.

When she opened the door to Saul's knock she saw him do a double-take, and inwardly hugged herself.

A shade drily, he remarked, 'You're looking very special.'

Wearing immaculate evening dress, he was as darkly handsome as any woman could have wished.

Resisting the urge to return the compliment, she said coolly, 'Thank you.'

It was a lovely evening, the clear, warm air giving a feel of lingering summer.

He took her to La Strada, the most exclusive restaurant on that stretch of the Thames. There were hothouse flowers for sale in the foyer. Roses, orchids, carnations...

He bought her a single exquisite red rose, and, for the first time in their relationship, treated her not as a familiar friend but as a desirable woman.

The food was excellent and the vintage champagne cool and crisp on her tongue, but, in the seventh heaven, Autumn wouldn't have cared if she'd been eating chaff and drinking water.

They were at the coffee stage when, having felt in his pocket, he muttered, 'Damn!'

When she looked at him, he said, 'I've forgotten your birthday present. The phone rang when I was about to put it in my pocket.'

She shook her head. 'I don't need a present. You've already given me so much.' But part of her happiness was dimmed, some sixth sense making her know the call had been from Joanna. Gritting her teeth, determined to sound casual, she asked, 'I take it Joanna's away?'

'Yes, she's working in Paris.'

So that was why he'd been free to take her out.

'On a long assignment?'

'A fashion romp scheduled to last a week. But she's managed to get home a day early, so I'm picking her up from the airport later tonight.' His voice was light but his grey eyes held a certain wariness, as though he half anticipated another jealous outburst.

'I expect you'll be glad to have her back?' Autumn forced herself to smile, to speak brightly, as if she didn't care.

'Yes, I will.' His answer was matter-of-fact, but his silvery eyes darkened with the flare of black pupils and his face appeared hewn out of granite.

He glanced at her, then quickly away again, but not before she'd seen the arousal in his eyes, the lick of flame that told of his desire for the other woman.

Now her evening was spoiled. And she'd only herself to blame.

Recalling what high hopes she had had for her eighteenth birthday, she wanted to cry. How easily Joanna, who had offered him only sex, had won.

While she, who could have given him everything, had let him go without a fight.

Trying to hold the bitterness at bay, she told herself not to be a fool. Harking back to that party would get her nowhere. In some ways she had still been a child then.

But she'd done a lot of growing up in the past three months. She wasn't a child any longer. She was a woman now, able to use a woman's weapons to fight for her man. And he was her man. He'd been hers before Joanna came on the scene, and he would be hers when Joanna had tired of him and gone...

'About ready to go?' His voice broke into her thoughts.

A daring idea beginning to take shape in her mind, she got to her feet without demur.

He appeared surprised, as though he'd expected her to want to linger.

Picking up her rose and her small evening-bag, she led the way to the door, bright head high, walking with the slightly coltish grace that came naturally to her.

On the drive back she sat quietly thinking, trying to dispel any last doubts. Surely, deep down, Saul did care for her? And this evening, while Joanna was still absent and his emotions made him vulnerable, might be the only chance she would ever get to force him to realise and acknowledge his true feelings...

After a glance at her absent expression, Saul drove without making any attempt to break the silence.

When they reached home he drew the car into his own driveway and made as if to take her next door.

'You said you had a present for me.' She sounded husky. Breathless.

'I'll see you home, then pop back with it.'

That wasn't part of her plan. Shaking her head, she began to walk to his front porch, saying gaily over her shoulder, 'Not likely, you might forget.'

With a little indulgent smile he followed her and, having unlocked the door, ushered her into the living-room.

Mrs Hawkins, his housekeeper, had left everything spick and span. There was a smell of lavender polish and freshly cut apple-logs. But it had been a warm September, and the tiled hearth was empty except for a tall vase of orange gladioli.

Seeing he was reaching for a small package on the sideboard, Autumn sat down in one of the big armchairs and said coaxingly, 'I'd love a drink to round off the evening.'

He raised a dark brow. 'What would you like?'

'A glass of wine,' she answered pertly, putting her evening-bag and the rose down on the coffee-table.

Looking amused, he agreed, 'Very well.' Discarding his jacket and bow-tie, he disappeared into the kitchen. She heard the sound of a cork popping and a moment or so later he returned, carrying a bottle of champagne and two glasses.

The wine was chilled to perfection, and Autumn guessed that it must have been intended to celebrate Joanna's return.

She drank it quickly and, needing Dutch courage, held out her glass for more.

He refilled it without comment.

This time she took it a little slower, but when she held out her glass for the second time he shook his head. 'I think you've had more than enough for one night.'

There he was, treating her like a child again. He wouldn't have said that to Joanna, she thought resentfully.

Seeing her scowl, he added, 'I don't want to have to carry you home.'

She wasn't intending to *go* home, but it was too soon to let him know that.

'Here—' picking up the gift-wrapped package, he tossed it into her lap '—open your present.'

Saul had always been generous, but in the past his presents had mostly been of an impersonal nature. Intuition told her that this one was different.

Tearing off the green-and-gold striped paper with fingers that shook slightly, she opened the black suede box, and gasped.

On a fine gold chain hung a magnificent opal pendant.
It was oval, and, beneath the dominant green, it glowed
with gold, orange and red, a breathtaking range of colours.
Autumn colours.

It banished the last lingering doubt. Deep inside, he *must*
care for her to have bought her such an exquisite and carefully chosen gift.

If only her plan would work, and she could get him to
make love to her, he would realise then that they belonged
together, and that all he'd felt for Joanna had been a passing
attraction...

CHAPTER FIVE

AUTUMN was still gazing down at the pendant, silent and absorbed, her long dark lashes like fans against her cheeks, when he said, 'There is a superstition that opals are unlucky, so, if you don't like it, feel free to choose something else.'

Looking up, her heart-shaped face radiant, she whispered, 'Oh, Saul, I *love* it. It's *beautiful*.' Lifting it from its velvet bed, she went to him. 'Won't you fasten it for me?'

She stood with her back to him, bright head bent a little, while he obliged. His fingers brushing her bare nape made her catch her breath and start to tremble.

The opal resting cool against her heated skin, she turned to face him. 'Thank you.' Standing on tiptoe, she put her arms round his neck and touched her mouth to his, her lips warm and velvety, a little parted.

After a second's hesitation he returned the soft pressure, causing her head to spin.

When he would have stepped back, her arms tightened, and she pressed her pliant woman's body to his hard male one. An innocent yet seductive temptress.

The resulting explosion was like dropping a lighted match into a pool of petrol.

Suddenly he was kissing her with a hungry passion which should have scared her. Instead, his kisses on her open, upturned mouth were sweeter than anything she could have imagined. They told her she was right, and drove away the last of her lingering inhibitions.

He was hers. She was his.

Clinging to him, she gave him kiss for kiss with a total abandonment, while her heart beat with a kind of fierce joy and the blood sang through her veins.

The zip at the back of her dress slipped down easily, leaving her clad only in her delicate lace-trimmed bra and panties.

A moment later Saul's hands were roaming over her lissom curves, measuring her slim waist, following the flare of her hips and buttocks and the long smooth length of thigh, before returning to release the clasp of her bra. He cupped her full breasts, his thumbs stroking the rosy nipples so that they firmed at his touch.

The sensations he was arousing were so exquisite that, burning with the kind of desire she had never even dreamt of, she whimpered softly in her throat.

Beneath her hands she could feel the fine cotton of his shirt, the small pearly buttons. Without conscious volition she began to undo them, pulling the fabric apart to touch his skin. It was warm and slightly moist, the sprinkling of crisp dark hair against her palms making them tingle.

Delighting in the experience, her untutored fingers explored the smooth collarbone, the lean ribcage, the strong ripple of muscles.

When he freed her lips to press kisses down the side of her neck and along one satiny shoulder, she nuzzled her face against his chest.

His skin smelled clean and wholesome, faintly spiked with the scent of shower-gel; it tasted of salt and sunshine and cologne. Her tongue-tip found and delicately teased one of the small, flat nipples, learning its shape and texture.

She heard his ragged gasp and realised with a heady rush of excitement that she could give him the same mind-blowing pleasure that he was giving her.

Suddenly, taking her completely by surprise, he thrust her away so violently that she stumbled and went down.

On her knees, eyes wide and startled, face still dazed and bemused by passion, she watched him run unsteady fingers through his dark hair and begin to re-button his shirt.

'What's the matter?' she whispered. 'What have I done? Oh, *please*, Saul…'

Breathing hard, he stared at her, crouching there like some beautiful half-naked supplicant. Then, his voice sounding hoarse, impeded, he said, 'It's not your fault. I should never have let it happen. Now, for God's sake, go and get dressed…' Almost to himself, he added, 'I ought to be starting for the airport very soon.'

Pierced to the heart, she gathered up her clothes and fled to the bathroom, the second door of which opened into Saul's bedroom. It was ajar, and the light filtering in from the bathroom gave her a glimpse of the large divan, turned down as though ready for its occupants.

If only things had been different, she thought passionately, she would have been sharing it with Saul. And when they'd made love, and were lying in each other's arms, he would have realised that it was *her* he loved, that what he'd felt for Joanna had been a mere infatuation…

But because the model was coming back a day too soon, everything had gone wrong…

Tears running down her cheeks, Autumn was struggling to fasten her bra with trembling fingers when she heard the front door slam.

She had just decided dully that it must be Saul leaving for the airport, when a voice she knew only too well called, 'Look who's here! Surprised to see me, darling?'

Saul's deeper tones answered, 'I certainly am. How come?'

Moving a little sideways, Autumn peered through the crack of the door. Joanna, tall and elegant, her blonde hair

in a sleek chignon, was dressed in a Paris suit that made
the new dress she'd thought so sophisticated look as though
it had been bought at a church jumble sale.

'Just minutes after I was talking to you,' the older
woman was saying, 'I found there was a seat on an earlier
plane. I tried to phone you back, but there was no answer.
When we landed at Heathrow I rang again. Still no answer,
so I took a taxi home and picked up my car.'

'I'm sorry I wasn't there to meet you.'

With a touch of irritability, Joanna demanded, 'Where
on earth have you been?'

'I was dining out.'

Her lips parted for his kiss, she was moving into Saul's
arms when her glance fell on the rose and the evening-bag.
She stopped dead in her tracks. 'And not alone, it seems.'

'No, I wasn't alone,' he replied evenly. 'It's Autumn's
birthday. Her parents are away so I took her out for a meal.'

'And brought her back here.'

'Only to collect her present.'

The sharp eyes rested on the black suede box. 'So you
gave her jewellery?'

'It's a special birthday.'

Her face full of anger and suspicion, Joanna demanded,
'Why have you suddenly started buying her things?'

'I haven't suddenly started. I bought her a birthday present when she was fourteen.'

'She's not fourteen any longer.'

'Granted. But she's always been quiet and shy, and because she's led a very sheltered life she's still extremely
young for her age.'

Staring at the half-empty bottle and the glasses, Joanna
snapped, 'But not too young to ply with champagne...
Were you planning to take her to bed?'

'No, I was not,' Saul said coldly.

'Well, you're a red-blooded man and I know how—'

His voice rough, he broke in, 'I keep telling you, she's a babe in arms…a mere child…'

How could he say that? Autumn thought bitterly. She was a woman now, offering him a deep and truly adult love. Offering him the kind of lifelong commitment that Joanna would never give him.

In control again, Saul was going on more smoothly, 'And you should know by now that inexperienced girls aren't to my taste.'

Joanna gave him a glinting look, then queried mockingly, 'So where is your poor little virgin hiding herself?'

After the briefest hesitation, Saul said, 'She's in the bathroom.'

'Well, for goodness' sake get rid of her. I can't understand why you waste your time and money on someone so hopelessly dull and naïve… I suppose you must feel sorry for her…'

When Saul said nothing, Joanna went on, 'Even if she was attractive and vivacious, you couldn't let yourself get serious about a girl with her background. She'll never belong in your class. I happen to know her father's parents entered the States as poverty-stricken Polish immigrants…'

Joanna's contemptuous words made Autumn cringe. It was true her now middle-class background couldn't compare with Saul's, but that hadn't seemed to worry him in the past.

Of course, Joanna would be more socially acceptable as his wife, but she didn't love him and she would never make him happy. Though at the moment Saul couldn't see that…

If only Joanna hadn't been coming back tonight… Autumn bit her lip hard. She had been so close to winning. So close to opening Saul's eyes…

But if she could get rid of Joanna now, once and for all, Saul would be hers and she could devote her life to making him happy…

Dropping the bra she was still holding, she stripped off her panties and, slipping into Saul's bedroom, switched on the light.

A cheval-glass briefly reflected back her hour-glass figure, and the opal pendant nestling just above creamy, pink-tipped breasts.

Giving herself no time to think of the possible consequences, she opened the door into the living-room, asking plaintively, 'Are you going to be much longer, darling?'

Two heads snapped round simultaneously.

Standing in the doorway, gleaming head held proudly, green-gold eyes jewel-bright, a tinge of apricot lying along each slanting cheekbone, she watched Saul's jaw drop, and felt a hysterical desire to laugh.

Taking in the long, slender legs, the flawless skin, the full, firm breasts and flaring hips that made the slim waist look even smaller, Joanna made a sound like a death-rattle.

'Some child!' Her face contorted with fury, she flew at Saul, striking at him, raking her long red nails down his cheek. 'You rotten, lying, two-timing Casanova…'

Spinning round, she rushed for the door, slamming it behind her so hard that the very air seemed to vibrate.

There was a dreadful silence.

Staring at Saul, Autumn watched the blood trickle down his white, set face with horrified eyes.

'What the *hell* do you think you're playing at?' His voice was quiet, lethal.

'I—I wanted to—'

He cut through her stammered words. 'Put your clothes on and go home. If you're still here when I get back I won't be responsible for my actions.' Turning on his heel, he started for the door.

Running to him, she caught his arm. 'No, no… Let her go… It's only her pride that's hurt. She doesn't really love you…'

'And I suppose you think you do?'

'Yes, I do,' Autumn cried defiantly. 'I've loved you all my life. She's only been using you, and I'm glad she's gone.'

'You silly, wilful child.'

'I wish you'd stop calling me a child. I'm *not* a child.' She threw her arms round his neck.

When he made as if to push her away she clung to him with all her strength, her face buried against his neck, her body pressed to his in deliberate provocation. 'Please don't go. I'm as much a woman as Joanna. I can give you everything she can and more...'

'So you want to take her place?'

'Yes... Oh, yes.' She pressed her lips to his throat, and felt him tremble.

Seizing her arms, his fingers biting in painfully, he held her away a little and, his voice hoarse with a combination of aroused passion and anger, grated, 'I'm warning you, I've had about as much as flesh and blood can stand. For the last time, will you get out of here?'

If she went now she'd have lost everything, including his friendship.

As soon as his grip slackened she clung to him once more, begging feverishly, 'Don't send me away. You wanted to make love to me, you know you did. Oh, *please*, Saul...' Her voice catching in a sob, she added, 'If it hadn't been for *her* we'd be in bed together now...'

His fury boiled over. 'Well, if that's what you want...' He swept her up into his arms and, striding through to the bedroom, tossed her on to the bed with scornful ease. 'Let's see how you like it.'

While he tore off his clothes she watched him with scared but fascinated eyes. She'd never before seen a naked man in the flesh, and the beauty and symmetry of Saul's lean-hipped, broad-shouldered body took her breath away.

Turning towards the bed, he seemed to hesitate momentarily. Terrified he was about to change his mind, with an instinct as old as Eve, she moved her hips enticingly and held out siren arms.

When his body came down on hers she accepted his weight gladly, winding her arms around his neck, her lips against the tanned column of his throat.

He took her without any preliminaries, stopping short of brutality, but allowing nothing for her utter inexperience.

After her first instinctive tensing against the pain, she gave everything she had to give, willingly, joyfully, and, when it was all over, cradled his dark head against her breast with a woman's tenderness.

Her heart overflowing with love, she waited for him to take her in his arms. Then, while she nestled against him, they could talk, and everything would miraculously come right.

But it didn't happen like that.

Pulling himself free, he rolled away and lay on his back, his eyes closed tightly, as though to shut out reality.

She turned towards him and, raising herself up on one elbow, pressed her lips to the bloody scratches running down his cheek.

He jerked away as though he found that soft touch unbearable, and, swinging his feet to the floor, sat on the edge of the bed, his back to her, his dark head in his hands.

'Saul…?' She said his name huskily, hesitantly.

His voice hoarse, he muttered, 'Oh, dear God!'

Here was no exultant lover, but a man in torment.

Suddenly afraid, she begged, 'Tell me what's the matter…what's wrong…?'

'Taking you to bed, taking advantage of your innocence, that's what's wrong. I'm nearly a decade older than you. I must have been out of my mind.'

'But I wanted you to…'

He turned on her, his face livid. 'You're just a child. Too young to know *what* you want.'

'D-don't be angry with me,' she stuttered. 'I do know, and I—'

'Angry with you!' His silvery eyes blazed. 'What else should I be after all you've done?'

Cowering away from his fury, she whispered, 'I'm sorry…I didn't intend to—'

'Don't give me that! Your actions were deliberate and wanton. Apart from provoking me into doing something I'm terribly ashamed of, you've probably lost me the woman I love.'

'No, no, you don't mean that,' Autumn protested. 'You *can't* love her…'

His mouth a thin line, he demanded, 'Who the hell are you to decide who I can and can't love?'

'But you've just made love to me,' she cried despairingly.

He laughed harshly. 'It's high time you learnt the difference between love and lust. What we did had nothing to do with love. That was sex, pure and simple…and I only wish to God it had never happened.'

Her humiliation complete, she whispered, 'Then you didn't even want me?'

'It would be hard for any red-blooded man not to want you,' he bit out. 'But I should have had a damn sight more self-control. By morning you'll be bitterly regretting it… And now I'm guilty of what Joanna suspected, it will probably wreck all my plans.'

'Your plans?'

'When I bought your opal, I also chose an engagement-ring.'

Her eyes big and startled, she breathed, 'An engagement-ring…?'

'Not for you,' he said with deliberate cruelty. 'Tonight I was going to ask Joanna to marry me.'

Every vestige of colour drained from Autumn's face. 'Marry you... But she—she's not the marrying kind...'

'You yourself pointed out that she was looking for a rich husband.'

In her pain, Autumn lashed out. 'Well, if a rich husband is all she wants she'll probably still marry you...'

His teeth snapped together. 'But it isn't all she wants. Whether you believe it or not, she loves me.'

As Autumn began to shake her head, he snarled, 'If she didn't, would she have been so angry and jealous when she thought I was two-timing her?'

'Well, she's no saint herself...'

'How do you know what she is or isn't?'

'I heard how she—'

Hands clenched into fists of rage, he broke in, 'You shouldn't believe all the malicious gossip you hear. Or did you *want* to believe it?'

That was so near the mark that Autumn flinched.

'You've always hated Joanna and been jealous of her— that was why you wanted to go to bed with me.'

'No, it was because I love you and I thought you loved me...' Tears began to run down her cheeks.

Balked of a physical expression of his fury, he lashed her with his tongue. 'You're too young and immature to know the meaning of the word love. All you wanted was to satisfy your sexual curiosity and make trouble between Joanna and me... Well, you should be pleased with yourself. You've succeeded on both counts. Now get out, you silly little fool!' His voice held savage contempt. 'Go on, run! Get out of my life and stay out. If I ever set eyes on you again we might both be sorry.'

Scrambling off the bed, she stumbled into the bathroom and, sobbing aloud, pulled on her clothes. She was reaching for the zip of her dress when she touched the chain around her neck.

Knowing she couldn't keep the pendant, she tried to unfasten it, but her trembling fingers were unable to undo the catch. In desperation, she took hold of the opal and tugged, feeling the pain as the thin gold chain bit into her flesh before snapping.

Dropping it on the coffee-table, she grabbed her bag and, blinded by tears, ran.

She had barely reached her own front porch when she heard a car door slam. A moment later Saul's Jaguar shot away from The Rowans with a squeal of tyres and sped down the quiet road.

So, in spite of all her hopes and dreams, it was Joanna he loved. Joanna he was going to marry. Unless in her blind and wanton stupidity she had ruined things for him.

In an agony of shame and remorse she wondered how she could have been so abysmally wrong. Made such a mess of everything.

She had thought then that her life was at its lowest ebb; she hadn't suspected there was much worse to come.

Next morning she'd heard of Saul's accident and, knowing she was to blame, had been shattered. Three days later, when she was told he'd lost his sight, she had wanted to die.

Even after four years, the anguish of that moment was still so intense that her hands were arrested on the piano keys and she sat motionless, as though mortally wounded.

'Don't stop.'

The soft injunction came with the shock of a blow, bringing her head up and making her heart lurch sickeningly.

Saul was lounging negligently in the doorway, eyes shielded by the tinted glasses, face sardonic above the black polo-necked sweater.

While she'd been reliving the past, the light had faded

and the room had grown dusky, but she could see his usually neat dark hair was still damp and, restyled by the wind
and snow, rumpled into ragamuffin curls and stray locks.

As she looked at him, a drop of melted snow ran down
his lean cheek. Recent memory turned it into a trickle of
bright blood.

'Do go on,' he urged. 'I've waited a long time to hear
you play.'

She began to shiver. 'I'm cold,' she whispered. And it
was the truth, but her coldness wasn't due solely to the
chill air.

'You should have lit the fire.' He made his unerring way
over to the hearth, where a large fire was already laid and
a supply of pine logs had been stacked in the alcoves.

Reaching on the stone mantel for a box of matches, he
struck one and applied it to the kindling.

It flared up with a fierce crackle and a shower of bright
sparks. Within seconds the wood had caught and begun to
blaze cheerfully, tongues of flame curling round the mas-
sive logs.

Turning, Saul remarked, 'That should soon warm the air,
but I suggest, until it does, we move back to the living-
room.'

Autumn needed no further prompting. Only too eager to
leave the uncomfortably evocative room, she jumped to her
feet, pushing back the carved piano-stool. As she put
weight on her injured ankle she gave an involuntary exclamation of pain.

'What's wrong?' he asked immediately.

'I slipped coming down the stairs and hurt my ankle.'

'Ah,' he said softly. 'I wondered why you hadn't made
a run for it.'

She straightened her shoulders. 'Suppose I had?'

'You wouldn't have got far.'

The silky menace made her shiver afresh. Gritting her teeth, she asked, 'What happened to the car?'

He smiled a little. 'Were you surprised to find it gone?'

'I suppose I should have expected it.' She spoke flatly, unwilling to add to his satisfaction.

'You should indeed. Especially when you found the keys I'd left for you.'

'How do you know I found the keys?'

'They were in the living-room with your case,' he answered blandly.

As he spoke he was moving towards her. Before she could guess his intention, he had stooped and scooped her up and was holding her against his broad chest.

She gave a startled gasp. 'What are you doing? I can manage.'

'Afraid I'll drop you? Don't worry, being blind doesn't mean I've lost my strength.'

'Oh, but I...'

'Put your arms around my neck,' he suggested, adding tauntingly, 'Don't be shy. You've done it before.'

Her heart beating so loudly that she felt sure he must hear it, she obeyed. One part of her revelled in his touch, his nearness, the other was afraid, scared both of his intentions and the emotions he could so effortlessly arouse in her.

Carrying her with ease, he made his way confidently to the door and through to the living-room.

After the cold, stressful atmosphere of the parlour it was comfortably warm and reassuring. The stove, newly made-up, burnt cheerily, lighting the gloom.

Instead of setting her on her feet, as she'd expected, he put her down on the couch in front of the fire, remarking, 'Better see how much damage has been done.'

A second or two later he had slipped off her shoes and socks and was examining her right ankle, which was now quite badly swollen. She winced as his lean fingers probed around the bone. After a moment he said, 'I think it's just a sprain—nothing seems to be broken.'

He went to the medicine-chest and returned with a crêpe bandage, soaked in something cold and aromatic, which he applied with a skilfulness that many a sighted person might have envied.

'Thank you,' she said, when he'd finished his self-appointed task.

'Verbal thanks are all very well—' she saw the cruel little twist to his lips '—but I'd hoped for something more…demonstrative.'

Her voice jerky, she said, 'I—I'm not sure what you mean…what you want…'

'Just a kiss.'

Hearing her little gasp, he asked derisively, 'Disappointed?'

Her chest feeling as though it was encircled by iron bands, she refused to answer.

Bending his head so that his beautiful mouth was only inches from hers, he waited.

Part of her wanted to kiss him, longed to kiss him, but, aware that he was baiting her, she remained quite still, her lips pressed tightly together.

After a long moment, he said with mock disappointment, 'No kiss? You were a great deal more forthcoming when I knew you last.'

Her heart thumping like a sledge-hammer, she stayed mute.

Straightening, he asked casually, 'I take it you haven't had anything to eat?'

'No, I'll…'

When she attempted to get up, he pushed her back. 'Stay where you are. We'll take pot-luck.'

Trying to gather her courage, to armour herself for the

confrontation to come, she watched him remove a prepared casserole from the freezer and put it in the microwave.

Leaving her place on the mat, Beth came over to the couch and put her handsome fawn and black head on Autumn's lap. Her coat was still slightly damp but it was obvious that, even if her master neglected himself, she had been towelled.

Autumn was stroking the dog, fondling the large, erect ears when Saul commented, 'You're honoured. She won't go to George like that, but she seems to have taken a fancy to you.'

'Two bitches together, perhaps.'

'You said it.'

'I was saving you the trouble.'

He grinned devilishly. 'So you've decided to fight back. Well, that should make things even more…interesting.'

The words themselves were innocuous, but there was an underlying relish that made her blood run cold.

'When did you realise who I was?' She stove to keep her voice level.

Taking cutlery from the drawer, he began to set a couple of trays with his usual deft efficiency before replying, 'My dear Autumn, I've known from the first.'

'I've known from the first…' The casual statement hit her like a blow to the solar plexus.

When she'd absorbed the shock, her voice hoarse, she asked, 'Then why didn't you say something sooner?'

Strolling over, he took a seat in one of the armchairs and, as though silently summoned, Beth went to sit at his feet. Running lean fingers over his chin, he said succinctly, 'I was enjoying the game…'

His answer, and the little smile that accompanied it, made her shiver.

'I had intended to play with you a bit longer, but once

I'd succeeded in getting you here I found I was impatient to—shall we say—go on to the next stage?'

He appeared to be looking straight at her, to be trying to gauge her reaction.

Though afraid of the answer, she still had to ask, 'What is the next stage?'

He smiled sardonically. 'Oh, to tell you that would spoil the fun. When I planned this—'

'I don't see how you could have planned it,' Autumn broke in. Then, doing her best to sound calm, unperturbed, she went on, 'You couldn't have known I was coming back to England. I didn't know myself until a few weeks ago.'

'As soon as you bought your air-ticket, I was informed.'

'You were having me spied on!' she accused.

'That's right,' he admitted calmly.

'Since when?'

'Shortly after you moved to New York I hired a firm of private detectives to keep you under surveillance.'

She stared at him open-mouthed. Then, her voice squeaking a little, she asked, 'Why?'

'When I was able to think straight, it occurred to me that you might be pregnant.'

'Oh...' She felt hot colour flood into her face. 'Well, I wasn't...' Then, in some agitation, 'So why have you paid to have me watched all these years?'

'I wanted up-to-date information on what you were doing, where you were living, your love-life, everything.'

'But why?'

'Who was it said, ''Knowledge itself is power''? At the risk of sounding melodramatic, I was waiting for the right time to force a reckoning, to take my revenge for the way you'd wrecked my life. The death of both your parents— among other things—made me decide this might well be it, so I made arrangements for when you returned to England.'

In a strangled voice, she asked, 'Supposing I hadn't returned?'

'I tried to ensure you would.'

'How?'

A log settled in a shower of sparks, and the glow turned his dark face into a bronze devil-mask. 'When I learnt you'd lost your job, I bought the brownstone your apartment was in so I could force you to leave...'

He smiled mirthlessly at her shocked silence, before going on. 'Luckily your engagement had ended, which saved me having to think of some way to break it up.'

Aghast, she protested, 'How can you talk so lightly about breaking up someone's engagement?'

'It's a pity you didn't think like that when you did your best to wreck mine.'

'But I had no idea you were going to be married. I thought...' Drawing a shaky breath, she changed tack. 'When I realised what I'd done I went to see Joanna and told her the truth.'

His dark head came up. In a strange voice, he said, 'That must have taken a great deal of courage.'

'I... It was the very least I could do.' Looking down at her hands, she whispered, 'I feel so bitterly ashamed.'

Harshly, he queried, 'Isn't it a bit late for remorse?'

'Isn't it a bit late for revenge?'

'*Touché.*' He made the gesture of a fencer acknowledging a successful riposte, then suggested, 'Let's both indulge ourselves. I went to a great deal of trouble to arrange everything...'

'How could you have arranged this...?' Her gesture encompassed not only the room but the whole situation. 'You couldn't be sure I would see that article in *Top People*, let alone act on it.'

'I couldn't be sure you'd *act* on it,' he agreed. 'But having arranged, through Gerald Baber, for the article to be printed, I made certain you'd see it.'

'Mr Davis…?'

'Was in my employ.'

She clenched her hands, the strong, slender fingers white at the knuckles, while she struggled to come to terms with how cleverly he'd manoeuvred her into his trap.

Finally, in a shaken voice, she said, 'To have gone to so much trouble you must want revenge very badly.'

'Oh, I do.'

Feeling as though a fine noose was tightening round her neck, she asked, 'Suppose I hadn't acted on it?'

He shrugged, his dark face impatient. 'Then I would have been forced to think of something else… Tell me, why *did* you? I got the distinct impression you had no intention of taking the job.'

'No, I hadn't,' she admitted. 'Well, not at first.'

'So why did you come to Gerald's office?'

'I—I wanted to see you again.'

'To crow?'

'How can you suggest such a thing?' she cried passionately. 'When I heard you'd been blinded, I…' She stopped, unable to go on.

'Did you cry for me, Autumn?' There was a razor-sharp edge to his voice.

'No.' It was the truth. She hadn't shed a single tear. Her grief had been too deep, too frozen by a glacial despair.

After a moment he asked curtly, 'So, why did you want to see me again?'

'I don't know,' she cried, a shade wildly. 'I just did.'

Dissatisfied, he persisted, 'You must have had some pressing reason to take such a risk.'

'I thought once I'd seen you I might be able to cut the ties with the past. Leave it behind me…'

'Instead, it's caught up with you.' Hearing her indrawn breath, he queried softly, 'Are you afraid?'

Lifting her chin proudly, she lied, 'No.'

'Then you should be.'

CHAPTER SIX

THERE wasn't the slightest doubt about the cold triumph, the purposeful implacability of those words.

Autumn's blood turned to ice.

Taking a steadying breath, she tried desperately to keep her voice from wobbling. 'You can't know how bitterly sorry I am for what happened. I'd make amends if I could, but I—I don't know what I can do....'

'You'll do anything and everything I want you to do.'

Suddenly the microwave buzzed, shattering the tense silence that had succeeded Saul's remark, and making Autumn jump violently.

'That sounds as though our meal's ready.' His attitude was relaxed now, almost pleasant.

Too worked up to think of food, she shook her head. 'I'm really not hungry. I'd rather—'

'We'll eat first and talk later.' His voice brooked no argument.

'Very well,' she agreed stiffly.

When she would have struggled up, he ordered crisply, 'Stay there. I'll get it.'

Rising to his feet, Saul checked the Braille watch he wore, and remarked, 'It must be nearly dark?'

'Yes.'

He turned on the standard-lamp, bathing her in a pool of light, while the rest of the room stayed shadowy. 'It isn't part of your punishment to have to sit in the dark,' he told her sardonically.

Trays on their knees, they ate in front of the stove, Saul with his usual healthy appetite, Autumn having to force down every mouthful.

She was scared, her throat tight with nervous apprehension, but she refused to let him see that, and she refused to give way to it.

After all, what could he *do* to her? No matter how angry and hostile he was, he wouldn't hurt her physically; she was still certain of that. Well, almost certain.

The old Saul would never have hurt anyone or anything weaker than himself, but this new, embittered man was still something of an enigma. He might be capable of anything.

No, no…she couldn't believe he would change so radically. She was safe from physical harm, and he could only get at her in other ways if she allowed him to. Her best defence was to stay cool and composed until he decided that enough was enough.

Although that was easier said than done…

When their plates were empty, he asked, 'Would you like anything else to eat?'

'No, nothing, thank you.'

He returned their trays to the kitchen area, remarking, 'I'll make some coffee.'

'I don't want any coffee,' she said raggedly.

'Sure?'

'Quite sure.'

'Then I suggest we go back to the parlour and you can play for me.'

Catching her breath, she stammered, 'I—I don't feel like playing tonight.' Thinking he might insist, she added in desperation, 'I can't use the pedals properly because of my ankle.'

His voice holding a kind of smooth menace, he said, 'In that case I'll have to devise some other form of entertainment.'

With a feeling of sick horror she realised she'd jumped out of the frying-pan into the fire. Whatever other form of entertainment he came up with, she wasn't going to like it, to say the least.

Before she could make any further protest, he swung her up into his arms and carried her through to the parlour, now warm and cosy, lit by the fire.

'You're shivering,' he observed, with what sounded remarkably like satisfaction. Having shouldered the door shut behind them, he settled her in one of the chairs by the blazing hearth, her bare feet on the thick sheepskin, and touched her cheek with a lean finger. 'Yet you don't feel cold.'

He smiled like a tiger when she flinched away.

She must get a hold on herself, Autumn thought frantically. It was playing into his hands to let him rattle her so badly.

Once she knew what he had in mind, not only for this evening, but for the rest of the time, she would feel better able to cope, she told herself shakily. It was the unknown that terrified her.

Taking the chair opposite, he leaned back, relaxed and easy, long legs stretched negligently in front of him, while silence filled the firelit room.

On the surface it was a scene of cosy domesticity, but tension, like strands of barbed wire, held her trapped and rigid.

Watching flames flicker on a face made inscrutable by dark glasses, she asked, as levelly as possible, 'How long do you intend to keep me at Farthing Beck?'

'You know the terms of our agreement.'

'So you do want me as a secretary?'

'Among other things.'

Something about the way he spoke made her lick her dry lips and ask unsteadily, 'What other things?'

'As chauffeur and cook, and to provide any other comforts I might need…'

The unmistakable implication in the words made the tiny hairs on her arms rise.

'I know you went away with your ex-fiancé, so I'm looking forward to finding out how much he managed to teach you about the art of pleasing a man.' Saul spoke with distant mockery.

Feeling as though every drop of blood had drained from her body, she protested, 'You're just trying to frighten me.'

Those cynical, unseeing eyes seemed to bore a hole in her. 'Why should that frighten you? There was a time you couldn't wait to jump into bed with me.'

'I was young and incredibly foolish.' Agitatedly, she added, 'And you weren't married then.'

'I'm not married now.'

'Not married!' she whispered. 'But I heard…'

He gave a wintry smile. 'At the last minute Joanna changed her mind.'

Oh, dear God, Autumn thought, as the realisation came that all this time he'd been alone. Her picture of him as at least having someone to love and support him had been a false one.

And the fact that Joanna had left him had been yet another thing to add to the score against *her*, to fuel his anger and hated, his desire for revenge.

'I'm sorry,' she whispered, only too aware how inadequate that sounded. 'I didn't know.'

'I believe she loved me as much as she was capable of loving anyone, otherwise she wouldn't have been so insanely jealous over you… But when it came to the crunch, she couldn't face the prospect of being tied for life to a blind man.'

Smoothly, he went on, 'So your scruples about me having a wife are quite unnecessary.'

He came to lean over her, making her mouth go desert-dry and her heart start to race. As she sat, motionless as any statue, he took her head between his palms and ran his fingers into her hair, playing with the thick, silky strands.

She saw the glint of his eyes behind the tinted lenses as he murmured, 'In some respects it's a pity your hair is so long. The night of your eighteenth birthday I remember it was cut very short, like a shining cap. It made your eyes look enormous and your neck like a swan's.' One hand freed itself to stroke lightly up and down her throat.

She shuddered, and his white teeth gleamed in a mirthless smile, before he went on, 'I've often thought about that night, and now I intend to—' A series of sharp barks cut through his words.

Saul straightened with a sigh. 'That's Beth wanting to be let out. I'd better take her for a walk before we go any further.'

Autumn released the breath she'd been unconsciously holding, and swallowed hard.

A glance at the window showed snowflakes being swirled against the dark glass. Fearful for his safety in the appalling conditions, she asked quickly, 'You won't be too long?'

'I hadn't realised you were so eager for my company,' he said sardonically. Then, with a wry twist to his lips, 'No, I won't be too long.'

A moment later the latch clicked behind him.

Grateful for the reprieve, however temporary, Autumn stared after his tall figure. There was a hollow feeling in the pit of her stomach and her mind was in a turmoil.

Saul had used the phrase, 'before we go any further...' How much further did he mean to go? she wondered anxiously. Was he just trying to scare her? Or was he really intending to take her to bed?

Remembering his kiss in the dark, the flame that had sprung up between them, she shivered.

Last time she had believed that deep down he cared for her. Now she knew he hated her, that all he wanted was to seduce her for his own satisfaction.

No, no, she couldn't, wouldn't, stay and chance that happening. Jumping to her feet, she began to struggle to the door. Somehow she had to get away before he came back.

She had pulled it open and stepped into the passage before common sense called a halt. Though the cold compress had worked wonders and her ankle felt a great deal better, it still wouldn't bear her full weight and, even if it had, to try and cross the moors on foot on a night like this was tantamount to suicide.

Closing the door again, she stood shaking, breathing with lungs that felt as though they were full of broken glass, while she conquered her panic and came to terms with her own helplessness.

When a few minutes had elapsed, having accepted the fact that she had to stay and face whatever was in store for her, she felt an almost fatalistic calm. It seemed this call to account, this reckoning, had been *meant*.

After all he'd suffered, perhaps Saul needed a chance to take his revenge, and perhaps *she* needed to feel she'd paid at least part of her debt.

In some strange way it might set them both free, enable them to slough off some of the bitterness and get on with their lives. Sever the ties. Strong ties that, in spite of four long years, still bound them to the past. And to each other.

Sighing, she brushed back a tendril of hair that opening the door had wafted across her cheek. As she did so she recalled Saul saying, 'It's a pity your hair is so long... I remember it was cut very short...'

Well, if that was how he wanted it... And wasn't cropping one's hair a sign of penitence...?

Without giving herself time to think, she took the scissors from the windowsill and began to hack at her thick, silky hair, the gleaming russet locks falling around her bare feet like autumn leaves.

She had only just finished, her hair standing up in soft spikes all over her head, the scissors still in her hand, when the door opened and Saul came in.

There was a striped towel slung around his neck and he was using one end to dry his dark head.

Autumn watched him silently: a lean, well-muscled man with wide shoulders, a trim waist and supple hips, whose height added symmetry and masculine grace.

When he discarded the towel and turned towards her, she saw he wasn't wearing his glasses and he appeared to be looking straight at her.

He took a single step and, with a harsh exclamation, stopped abruptly, his look scorching her like a white-hot blast from a furnace. But those burning eyes held not only fury, but *awareness*.

As the incredible fact sank in, Autumn stood rooted to the spot, her eyes great dark pools in a face totally drained of colour.

'What in hell's name have you done to yourself?' Saul demanded savagely. 'Why have you cut your hair?'

She saw his lips move without hearing his words as the scissors fell from her nerveless fingers, a roaring filled her ears, and blackness rose up to meet her.

When she opened her eyes it was to find herself in the armchair with Saul bending over her. For a moment or two she looked up at him, dazed, before recollection came flooding back.

'You can see,' she breathed. 'Oh, Saul, you can *see*... Thank God... Oh, thank God,' she whispered, while tears began to run unheeded down her cheeks.

His hard face didn't soften. 'If you imagine that puts everything right, think again.'

'I don't…of course I don't, but I—'

An arm each side of her, trapping her there, his dark face only inches away from hers, he sliced through her faltering words with barely contained fury. 'Why have you cut your hair?'

'I thought you wanted it short—wanted me to cut it…' Then, with a flash of spirit, 'Surely you approve of an act of penance?'

'You silly little fool,' he snarled, and, his face contorted with something akin to anguish, stroked his hand over her shorn head. 'I could cheerfully put you across my knee for ruining your beautiful hair.'

Staggered by the violence of his reaction, she stammered, 'It—it doesn't matter…it'll grow again.'

'I've a good mind to beat you every day until it does…' Almost to himself, he added, 'Since I saw you in Baber's office, I've been wanting to play with it, wanting to spread its perfumed silk over my pillow and bury my face in it until I was as dizzy as a bee drunk on nectar…'

His grey eyes had darkened and grown sensuous, as if he'd withdrawn to some secret place where imagination was more real than reality.

After a few moments he shook himself, banishing the introspection, before allowing his hand to slide down the creamy skin of her throat, his index finger coming to rest lightly against the pulse at the base.

As it began to race betrayingly, he proposed, with quiet intent, 'Time for a glass of wine, don't you think?'

Thrown completely off-balance, distrusting that loaded suggestion and the little smile which accompanied it, she hesitated before agreeing reluctantly, 'If you like.'

'That's my girl.' Picking up her hand, he lifted it to his lips and kissed the palm, then, turning it a little, bit the mound of her thumb just hard enough to make her give a choking gasp before releasing it.

Pausing on his way to the door, he picked up the scissors and, tossing them back into the windowsill, drew the curtains against the snowy night.

Using her fingers to wipe cheeks stiff with drying tears, she watched him disappear into the passage, while all the time anxious conjectures tore holes in the flimsy fabric of her self-possession.

Only seconds later, as though everything had been ready and waiting in the wings like stage props, he returned with a bottle of champagne and two glasses and put them on the low table.

Easing out the cork with a pop, he poured the still-smoking wine and handed her a glass.

Since the night of her eighteenth birthday she had assiduously avoided drinking champagne. It brought back far too many disturbing memories.

Now, with a nerve-racking feeling of *déjà vu*, she watched the golden bubbles slowly rising to the surface, and listened to the soft fizz.

'Aren't you going to drink it?' he prompted.

Unwillingly, yet as though compelled, she began to sip. The wine was deliciously cool and crisp, with just a hint of sweetness. Her suspicions were making her on edge and wary; it could have been vinegar.

As soon as her glass was empty he leaned forward to refill it. Shaking her head, she protested, 'No more, thank you.'

He raised a dark, mocking brow. 'Don't tell me you've lost your taste for champagne? I remember on your eighteenth birthday you couldn't get enough of it.'

When, head down, she stayed silent, he replaced the bottle, and remarking, 'I've been keeping this for you,' tossed a small flat box into her lap.

Autumn froze into immobility, knowing now that her suspicions had been correct. This was a deliberate and carefully staged re-enactment of that night four years ago.

When she continued to sit and gaze blindly at it, he said, 'Open it.' It was an order, curt and unequivocal.

Pressing the catch with her thumb-nail, she opened the lid with unsteady fingers. Though it was what she had expected to see, shock still exploded inside her.

'Would you like me to fasten it for you?'

'No!' she exclaimed hoarsely. 'I don't want it on.'

'Oh, but I insist. I had it mended especially.'

Stricken, she begged, 'Please, Saul, don't make me wear it.'

'When I first gave it to you, you said that it was beautiful, that you loved it.'

'*You* said, ''There's a superstition that opals are unlucky''...'

'But I don't believe in superstition,' he said adamantly.

Taking the opal from its box, he moved behind her. When he'd fastened the fine gold chain around her neck, his hand slid beneath her chin and forced her head back, so that she found herself looking into his dark face, intriguingly inverted.

'Aren't you going to thank me? Give me a kiss as you did last time?'

'Why are you doing this?' she choked. 'Why do you want everything to be exactly the same? Tell me why.'

He released her abruptly and went to sit in the chair opposite. With a grimace of self-contempt at his own weakness, he admitted, 'All these years the memory of that night has haunted me. Let's say I think you owe me a re-run, if only to dispel the ghosts.'

'But now you've got your sight back...'

'That doesn't wipe the slate clean,' he stated coldly. 'In fact, getting my sight back is what's made the time right for a reckoning... And you've a great deal to answer for. Almost four years spent in total darkness is a long while.'

Having suffered vicariously, she didn't need to be told. Striving to keep her voice level, dispassionate, she asked, 'How long have you been able to see?'

For a moment she thought he was going to ignore the question, then he said abruptly, 'Almost three months. I had a series of operations and, just when I'd almost given up hope, the last one proved successful.'

He turned his head slightly and fire-glow lit the side of his face. For the first time she noticed on his temple a network of scars like pale threads of cotton. Huskily she asked, 'Will you need to wear glasses permanently?'

He shook his head. 'Only for a limited period, and when the light is fairly strong.'

'Saul...why did you pretend to be still blind?'

'For obvious reasons it was necessary at first.' With fierce satisfaction, he added, 'I was enjoying playing out this charade, and I'd intended to keep up the pretence a little longer, but then I had second thoughts.

'You see, the last time you took your clothes off I wasn't in the right frame of mind to appreciate it. So when I decided to make you strip again for my pleasure, it occurred to me that I'd get a lot more satisfaction out of it if you knew you were stripping for a sighted man rather than a blind one.'

Green eyes lifted to meet grey with an unspoken plea. They met only cold mockery.

His deep, attractive voice became lower, slightly husky. 'What happened that night seemed branded into my brain. I retained a vivid picture of how you looked standing naked in the doorway with just that pendant lying above your breasts...'

What she read in his dark face made her swallow hard. Instantly his eyes fell to the smooth column of her throat before lifting again to meet hers. She went hot at the hunger she saw reflected in that sensual gaze.

'Desire and hatred make a potent and disturbing combination,' he continued softly. 'I'd lie awake for hours in the darkness and imagine all the things I'd like to do to you...'

A kind of panic brought her to her feet.

'Sit down.' Though quietly spoken it was an order.

Ignoring his command, she attempted to run. Instantly he was by her side, lightly encircling her wrist.

When she tried to jerk free his long fingers tightened around the slender, deceptively fragile bones. They went on tightening relentlessly until the pain made her gasp, and she stopped struggling and sat down abruptly.

'Now you're showing sense,' he murmured mildly.

He was teaching her a lesson, she realised, making it clear that he was the master and it would pay to obey him.

Releasing her wrist, he ran a hand over her down-bent head. A strange note in his voice, he said, 'You look just like a kitten whose fur has been stroked the wrong way.'

With a touch of grim humour, she muttered, 'Keep that in mind. I've never known you to be unkind to dumb animals.'

He laughed and remarked approvingly, 'I much prefer you with spirit. It will make subduing you a great deal more...entertaining.'

'You must be—' The choked words stopped abruptly.

'Mad?' he supplied. Then, thoughtfully, 'Not quite, though I may well have got close to it at times.'

And she couldn't blame him. All too clearly she could see how anger and bitterness, pain and frustration, must have almost driven him out of his mind.

Seeing her shiver, he added with a ruthless smile, 'Over the past four years the thought of having you at my mercy,

to do with as I pleased, has become something of an obsession…'

Though the years hadn't been easy for her, what she had
suffered was nothing compared with the problems he'd had
to face. And was still facing.

He might be able to see again, but it was clear that,
before he could be free of the past and really start living
once more, he had somehow to get this obsession out of
his system.

As though reading her thoughts, he asked, 'Do you know
the best way to rid oneself of an obsession, Autumn?'

When she stayed silent, he went on, 'As quite a young
child I developed a passion for cake and chocolate and
refused to eat anything else. Instead of smacking me, my
mother, being a woman of initiative, fed me chocolate at
every meal for days on end until I was sickened of it…'

She stared at him, her eyes wide and dark, her face pa-
per-white.

His smile was mocking. 'In your case, I don't know how
long it will take to sate myself…' Seeing her shudder, he
added, 'But the knowledge that you're hating every minute
of it will add immeasurably to my pleasure…'

For a moment she thought she was going to lose consciousness again. Head bent, the blood pounding in her
ears, she held back an abject plea only with an effort of
will so strong she could concentrate on nothing else.

If she'd hated him it would have been bad enough, but,
loving him as she did, how could she bear to have him
seduce her only to throw her aside when he tired of her?

But if it would set him free, then surely she owed him
that much…

Lifting her bright head, she looked him in the face. Frigid
grey eyes read her acquiescence and gleamed with cold
triumph.

'Don't look so martyred,' he mocked. 'Once you were

excessively eager to take Joanna's place. Now I'm giving you the chance…though I rather doubt if you've learnt enough to be able to excite a man the way she could.'

'I doubt it too,' Autumn informed him, with a flash of temper.

He raised a dark brow. 'Well, well… So my kitten has claws. Were you thinking of using them on me?'

She shook her head. 'I leave that kind of thing to women like Joanna.'

His lips twisted in a grim smile. 'Still jealous, I see.'

'No,' Autumn said tiredly, 'just angry at the way she left you.' It wasn't completely true. Deep in her heart, she would always feel a painful envy that it was Joanna he had loved and wanted to marry rather than her.

'You were jealous once, when you imagined you loved me.'

'I didn't imagine it.'

'Oh, come now! You were too young and green to know what love was all about. Apart from jealousy, all you felt was a combination of hero-worship and sexual curiosity, wasn't it?'

'No,' she denied simply. 'I loved you.'

A strange glitter in his eyes, he pointed out, 'If what you felt had really been love, it would have lasted.'

Unable to argue against that simple logic, she sat silent.

With the speed of a striking cobra, he asked, 'So are you saying you still love me?'

She bit her soft inner lip until a trickle of blood ran into her mouth, warm and salty. To admit the truth would give him a whip to flay her with. Mutely she shook her head.

Cynically, he observed, 'I hardly thought so. In fact I know your so-called love died a very swift death. Though after the accident your conscience apparently troubled you, you didn't even cry for me, and when I—' His white teeth snapped together, biting off the bitter, condemnatory words.

'However,' he went on more temperately, 'it isn't your love I want, it's your delectable body... Just for the record, Autumn, how many other men have enjoyed it?'

'Don't tell me your detective didn't keep you informed?' she asked mockingly.

'Your ex-fiancé was the only one he seemed to know about.'

With truth, she said, 'I guess I'm just a one-man woman.'

'Did you love him, Autumn?'

'Why else would I have been going to marry him?'

'There are other reasons. Why did you break up?'

'We weren't really suited.'

'Did you go to bed with him?'

'You asked that before.'

'And you refused to tell me, so I'm asking again and this time I want an answer.'

Lifting her chin, she lied coolly, 'Yes, of course. As you yourself pointed out, it's practically the norm these days.'

His face was impassive, and she was unable to judge whether or not that had been the answer he'd wanted. Curtly, he queried, 'How many times?'

'I'm afraid I didn't keep count,' she said sweetly, 'but as often as we could. Richard was a very sexy man.'

Saul scowled. 'In that case, I don't have to worry about you being inexperienced.'

'You didn't worry about it last time.' The words were out before she could prevent them.

A second later he was looming over her, and for one dreadful moment she thought he was going to strike her.

As she watched him clenching and unclenching his hands, visibly fighting for self-control, she felt a fierce satisfaction. He might be stronger physically, but he wasn't going to have things all his own way.

'You'd better watch your tongue,' he said tightly, while

a muscle jerked in his jaw. 'If I lose my temper you may regret it.'

'I regret a lot of things,' she told him wearily.

'So you should. You owe me, Autumn, and you're going to pay your debt. It shouldn't be too hard. I don't want love or affection, all I want is the use of your body.'

'You can have it, if it gives you any satisfaction. But that's all you'll get. I won't let you break me.'

At the bitter, desperate words, some powerful emotion glittered in the implacable gaze he bent on her, but all he said was, 'We'll see. After a while you may not be quite so confident... Now, suppose you start by undressing for me.'

'Well, of course, if you need titillation...'

She saw the flash of his eyes, then he taunted, 'Before you provide it, perhaps you'd like some more champagne?'

About to refuse, she thought better of it. If she was a little drunk it might help to make the ordeal easier.

Reading her expressive face, he filled a glass and handed it to her.

Her eyes on the other glass, she asked, 'Aren't you having any?'

He smiled derisively. 'You may need more. And I'd prefer to keep a clear head.'

Wanting to get the whole thing over, knowing that to prevaricate would only make things worse, she swallowed the wine so fast that she choked, and for a few seconds coughed and spluttered helplessly.

When the glass was empty he refilled it, suggesting sardonically, 'Take it a little slower this time. I don't want you to pass out on me.'

If only she could... But she knew quite well there was no escape that way.

Resuming his seat, he leaned back comfortably, crossing his legs at the ankle. Waiting.

Having swallowed the last of her wine, she replaced the glass and got up carefully, her weight on her good foot.

It was the work of a moment to pull her jumper over her head and discard her skirt. Standing in her delicate, semi-transparent ivory undies, a flag of bright colour flying in each cheek, she hesitated.

'Take your time,' he said, looking her over with all the insolence of a sultan visiting a slave-market. 'I prefer to take my pleasures slowly…savour them.'

She had been hoping against hope that he would call a halt, but it was painfully clear that he intended to have his pound of flesh.

Hoarsely, she asked, 'Do you hate me so much?'

'What do you think?'

Teeth clenched until her jaws ached, and remembering that long-ago night with a burning sense of shame, she took off her slip, and, unfastening her bra with icy-cold fingers, tossed it aside.

The opal caught the firelight and gleamed against her faultless skin.

She heard Saul release his breath in a sigh, then, his eyes fixed on her breasts, he said slowly, 'The years have improved you, Autumn. You're even more beautiful than I remember.'

Though her cheeks were scarlet as Judas-flowers, with the stony calm of despair she stood straight and proud while he looked her over, her hands by her sides, her head held high.

Tall and slender, with elegant lines, her body now had a lithe and graceful rather than a voluptuous sensuousness. Her face had always held a rare and haunting beauty and the intervening years had added character and strength. Only her mouth showed a touching vulnerability.

When, his leisurely inspection finished, she made no further move, he asked, 'Were you intending to stop there?'

Somehow she found her voice. 'No… But you said you preferred to savour your pleasures slowly.'

With a gleam of respect in those grey eyes, he saluted her spirit.

Using her will-power as a whip, she was about to divest herself of her dainty panties when he said abruptly, 'Leave them,' adding in a lighter tone, 'I need something to take off.'

As she turned slightly and the firelight gilded her skin, he jumped to his feet and came closer. Lifting her right arm to examine her ribs, he demanded, 'Where the hell did you get all those bruises?'

'My ankle gave way and I fell on the cobbles.'

'Then I'll have to be careful how I handle you.'

The words held a deliberate arrogance, and her soft mouth tightened.

His glance dropping to her bandaged foot, he said silkily, 'And you've been standing on that long enough. I suggest you take the weight off it. The rug's nice and thick and you'll be a great deal more comfortable lying down.'

CHAPTER SEVEN

As EVERY trace of colour drained from Autumn's face, leaving it white and pinched, Saul said abruptly, 'You don't need to worry. I've no intention of hurting you.'

Not physically, perhaps. And if she'd hated him she could have somehow coped with being used against her will. But, loving him as she did, even if he was gentle with her body, he could crucify her mentally and emotionally.

Thinking how different it might have been if only he'd loved her, she closed her eyes against the pain.

Abruptly, hoarsely, he said, 'For God's sake, don't look like that!'

Slowly, with an effort of will that left her limp, she smoothed the lines of anguish into a blank mask.

Lifting a hand, he tilted her chin. She looked down, so that all he could see were thick dark lashes lying like fans on her cheeks, and the line of her lips pressed tightly together to stop them trembling.

With an incoherent murmur, he bent his head and touched his mouth to hers, the tip of his tongue brushing her lips to part them.

The sensation was so startlingly erotic that, shuddering, she jerked away, crying, 'Don't.'

'Then co-operate...' He drew her back into his arms.

Though she wanted to pay her debt, she couldn't bring herself to do it willingly, generously, to abandon herself to him. She didn't want to lose her pride or her self-control. Didn't want to leave herself defenceless.

And because he didn't love her, his lovemaking was exquisite torture. If he would be satisfied with just *taking* her...

Feeling her rigidity, he coaxed, 'It won't be like last time, you know. I won't rush you. We'll take it slowly, wait until you're ready—'

'I'll never be ready,' she broke in hoarsely. 'And I don't want to "take it slowly". I'll suffer it, but I want to get the whole thing over as quickly as possible...'

Angrily, he said, 'If you imagine I'm going to allow you merely to "suffer" it...'

'How can you stop me? I know it would boost your ego if I did respond, but I won't. Nor will I actively resist. If I fought tooth and nail, you might feel justified in raping me, and I've no intention of making things easy for you...'

'And I've no intention of raping you. Nor do I mean to let you lie beneath me like some wax doll. I made a mistake in thinking that all I wanted was your body. Even if I don't get active participation, I want—intend to have—a response. Open your mouth for me, Autumn.'

Mutely she shook her head.

Holding on to his patience, he said, 'I've no idea what kind of lover your ex-fiancé was, but, if you stop this foolishness and let yourself respond, you might find you enjoy my lovemaking.'

'I don't want to enjoy it,' she announced tightly. 'And I don't know how you can use the term *lovemaking*. Lust is all it is.' Bitterly, she added, 'I just wish I'd stayed on the other side of the Atlantic.'

'Autumn—' he began.

'It's all right,' she broke in, her voice polite and distant now, under control. 'I know I owe you, and I intend to pay my debt. But I won't take an active role and I won't pretend to enjoy it.'

Lifting her head, she looked him in the face. 'You won't get much pleasure from a reluctant partner.'

'Then I'll have to make quite sure you don't stay reluctant,' he said grimly. 'Make sure you give—'

'The only thing I'm prepared to give,' she interrupted coldly, 'is a dutiful passivity.'

She was deliberately trying to rile him, preferring his anger to his lust, innocently unaware that one could be expressed by the other.

But instead of angry, he sounded wryly amused as he remarked, 'I think I prefer open rebellion to "dutiful passivity". Rebellion I can cope with—'

She laughed bitterly. 'Oh, I'm sure you can. A big strong man like you. But can you cope with making love to a statue?'

'We'll have to see, won't we? So why don't you lie down? Practise a spot of this "dutiful passivity".'

Infuriated by his mockery, wishing she'd never used those words, she knew there was no way she could spread-eagle herself naked at his feet.

Perhaps if he weren't fully clothed she wouldn't feel at quite such a disadvantage, she thought resentfully.

Catching her glance, and reading her expressive face, he suggested, 'You're quite at liberty to take them off,' adding, with a wicked grin, 'I promise I won't struggle.'

He took a step towards her and when, involuntarily, her hands went behind her back, he laughed.

'You're enjoying this,' she accused unsteadily.

'Of course. That was the whole idea… Ah, well, if you refuse to co-operate…'

With a sudden movement that took her by surprise he neatly hooked her good foot from under her, and she found herself ignominiously flat on her back.

Standing tall and arrogantly male, he stripped off the black sweater. Her eyes were irresistibly drawn to the smooth ripple of muscles and the sprinkle of crisp dark hair that arrowed towards his flat stomach.

His shoulders and chest were broad, his waist and hips narrow; his clear, healthy skin gleamed like oiled silk in the firelight. As his hands dropped to the waistband of his trousers, she looked everywhere but at him her mouth suddenly dry.

When he joined her on the rug she shut her eyes tightly and turned her face away.

'Would you be more comfortable with a cushion under your head?' he asked solicitously.

'No,' she answered through gritted teeth.

The moment he touched her, although the rug was thick and fleecy and her skin was warmed by the fire, she began to shiver.

He covered her face and throat with soft baby kisses, pressing them on her closed eyelids and temples, following the pure line of cheek and jaw.

His touch light as thistledown, he brushed her mouth with his own, pausing to stroke the hollow beneath her lower lip with his tongue. The novel caress made her heart lurch crazily.

Warm on her nape, his hand cradled the back of her head while he teased her tightly closed lips until they parted a little and the tip of his tongue was able to explore the moist, sensitive skin inside her short upper lip.

Though her very bones seemed to melt, she struggled to resist his skilled lovemaking.

While he kissed her persuasively, he slid the dainty panties over her hips and discarded them before stroking and lightly tugging the silky nest of russet curls.

She gave a choking gasp and went rigid.

'Still determined to fight?' he asked softly.

Lifting himself away, he sat down behind her, a muscular leg each side of her hips, and, pulling her against his chest with one arm, used the other hand to tip her head back so that it rested on the juncture of his bare shoulder and upper arm.

With the advantage of surprise he forced open her lips and, making her tilt her head to accommodate his wishes, explored her mouth with a slow, sensuous appreciation which, despite all her efforts to stay cool, sent her heart racing wildly and heated her blood.

While her stomach clenched and every nerve in her body sang into life, he kissed her with consummate skill, forcing her mouth open more fully as the provocative seconds passed.

She thought nothing could be more erotic, until his hands found her breasts, stroking them with his fingers, weighing them in his palms.

The dusky-pink nipples firmed beneath his touch, and when he began gently to tease them between his fingers and thumbs, her body jerked betrayingly.

Making a soft, satisfied sound in his throat, he freed her mouth and, his dark head close to her bright one, his lips brushing her ear, whispered, 'You like that, don't you, Autumn?'

She refused to answer.

As punishment, he nipped her lobe with his white teeth, bringing a small cry of protest.

Alternating kisses with a tantalising sucking and nibbling, which made her gasp and squirm, his mouth travelled over the smooth skin of her neck and shoulders, the slight rasp of stubble only adding to the stimulation.

Then, holding her upper arms, he traced the hollow of her spine, his tongue following the slight bumps and indentations almost down to her buttocks, then back up again.

Her entire body seemed nothing but a tingling mass of nerve-endings when his hands slid over her ribs once more and came to rest on her diaphragm.

Gripped by the most intense excitement she'd ever known, she found herself holding her breath, waiting for him to touch her breasts, longing to feel those piercingly sweet sensations again.

Aware of her tension, he leaned forward and, putting his cheek against hers, asked softly, 'What is it, Autumn? What do you want? You'll have to tell me.'

'I—I don't...'

When he suddenly took his hands away, she made a small choked sound in her throat.

'Disappointed?'

'Saul...' It was a plea.

He moved suddenly and, laying her down again, came to stretch full length beside her. This time, when he bent his dark head to kiss her mouth, it opened under his like a flower opened for the sun.

While he kissed her with a sensuous sweetness, his hand teased and tantalised, moving over her body with a leisurely thoroughness, measuring her slim waist, following the curve of her hip, stroking across her flat stomach, discovering the soft, silky skin of her inner thighs.

Once again she tensed, finding herself waiting, longing...

But, making her wait, intensifying that ache of anticipation, his hand stilled and his mouth began to make the same erotic journey, down and back.

When it reached her breasts, his tongue found and played with first one hard nipple, then the other. She gave a kind of gasping sob, and her hands came up to hold his dark head against her breast.

He began to suckle, softly, sweetly, tugging a little, stroking with his tongue. The sensations he was causing were so intense, so needle-sharp, that she wondered how much she could stand of such delightful torture.

One hand had moved downwards, seeking and finding,

and his long, lean fingers were bestowing a rhythmic stimulation.

While his mouth and hand kept up their sensual onslaught, he used the fingers of his free hand to pleasure her other breast, sending shafts of fire to meet the melting fire deep in the pit of her stomach.

The excitement and the feeling intensified until, mindless, lost to everything but what he was doing to her, she began to whimper softly in her throat.

He kissed her then, taking the little sounds into his mouth with all the pleasure of a conqueror, before lifting his head to say, 'Tell me you want me, Autumn.'

Through half-closed lids she glimpsed the passion and hunger in his dark face, and breathed, 'Yes... Yes, I want you.'

Though the words were barely audible, he seemed satisfied.

When he lowered himself into the cradle of her hips, Autumn, forgetting everything but her overwhelming love for him, accepted his weight gladly, glorying in it.

There was none of the shame or humiliation she had feared. They weren't master and slave. For that moment, at least, their mutual need made them equals, and somehow that made everything right.

She gasped at his first hard thrust, and for a moment he tensed and seemed to hesitate.

Terribly afraid he was going to pull away and leave her, she put her arms around his neck and lifted her hips in a way instinct told her would incite him.

He groaned her name and began to move again, more slowly and with care. She sighed raggedly and, her eyes shut tight, her lips pressed against the strong column of his throat, moved with him, blindly, instinctively.

The spiralling sensations grew and intensified, building up like a relentless crescendo, focusing all her concentration, until her whole being seemed to explode in a glorious sunburst of colour. Then she was tumbling into blackness, gasping and sobbing, her body racked by an ecstasy so far beyond anything she could have imagined that she thought she might die.

Only then did he relax his iron control and allow himself to fall with her into the abyss.

As the mists cleared a little, Autumn became aware of Saul's weight still pinning her down. He lay motionless, his eyes closed, his breath coming fast, his heart pounding so hard it seemed to shake her body.

Silently crying, Oh, I love you...I love you, she cradled his dark head against her breast while the euphoria induced by his lovemaking lapped around her like a warm tide.

Gradually, both his and her heartbeat and breathing returned to a more normal rate and Autumn's euphoria faded, to be replaced by a deep melancholy tinged with shock. So that was it, the 'little death' that no amount of words seemed able to describe adequately.

She had never expected to know it, nor had she expected to feel this overwhelming sadness after the most shatteringly beautiful experience of her life.

But, no matter what the future held, Saul had given her a gift beyond price. Tears crept beneath her closed lids and trickled down her face, leaving shiny tracks of wetness.

Perhaps she made some sound, because he raised his head, then his weight lifted from her. There were sounds of movement, as though he was pulling on his clothes. A moment or two later she heard the door open and close.

Surely he hadn't gone?

She sat up and looked around the shadowy room; it was empty. In spite of all they had just shared he'd left her without a single word.

Drained, emotionally spent, she sat where she was, knees

drawn up, forehead resting against them, her skin warmed by the fire-glow while a paralysing coldness spread inside.

This was what it would feel like when he eventually left her, only much, much worse.

The knowledge that she could respond so intensely was a mixed blessing. On one hand, her doubts as to whether she could ever have a satisfactory sexual relationship had been dispelled, on the other, it made her feel even more vulnerable.

While only too aware that it would crucify her emotionally, she had thought she could let Saul make love to her and remain physically unmoved, safe from the extremes of sexual excitement.

Now she knew she could not. If she stayed with him, by the time his obsession was over, she would be a burnt-out shell.

But she'd promised him recompense, agreed, in principle, to do whatever he asked. So what option had she? Unless she could appeal to his—

Without warning the door opened and Saul came in, carrying a round tray which held two glasses a quarter full of amber liquid.

For a moment she sat paralysed, the firelight turning her eyes to emeralds and making the opal glow with a wonderful range of colours against her gilded skin.

As he put the tray down on the table, Autumn, flustered because she was still naked, scrambled to her feet and reached for her clothes.

'Don't bother getting dressed. Put these on.' Over his arm he had her night-things.

'Thank you.' She pulled the nightdress over her head with undignified haste and struggled into the dressing-gown, tying the belt, knotting it twice.

He watched the hurried movements with sardonic amusement.

When she was settled in her chair he offered her a glass, remarking, 'You looked as if you could use a brandy.'

Hating spirits, she accepted it nevertheless, needing something to do with her hands, something to hide behind.

Saul sat down opposite and, though she avoided looking at him while she sipped, coughing a little as the raw liquor burnt her throat, she was nerve-rackingly aware of his steady, unwavering regard.

As soon as her glass was empty she replaced it on the tray and, desperate to get away from that too-searching inspection, said as steadily as possible, 'If you don't mind, I'd like to go to bed.'

'Of course I don't mind.' Eyes gleaming, he added, 'I think it's an excellent idea. Now the ice has well and truly melted, I don't want to give it time to re-form.'

'Saul, please...I can't go on with this. I *can't*... Please don't make me.'

He sighed. 'You certainly pay your debts none too willingly.'

She heard the edge of contempt in his voice and flushed.

'You didn't really mean to go through with it at all, did you?' he accused her.

'I did mean to...but then I...'

'Decided to try freezing me off.'

She sat head down, the firelight casting the shadows of her long lashes on to her cheeks, her shorn hair making her look oddly vulnerable.

'Why so reluctant, Autumn? What happened to that eager girl who couldn't wait to jump into bed with me?'

'Then I thought... I really thought...'

'You thought you loved me.'

The derision in his voice brought her head up. 'I thought *you* loved *me*...'

Momentarily he looked jolted, then he said flatly, 'I

didn't believe you then and I don't believe you now. You knew all about my relationship with Joanna.'

'Of course I knew, but...' Vainly, she tried to explain. 'I believed that what you felt for Joanna was just—just physical... Infatuation rather than love.'

She hesitated, then, swallowing hard, went on in a rush, 'I know now I was hopelessly wrong, but at the time I had this stupid conviction that you and I belonged together. I wanted you to realise it too...'

Perhaps it was the effects of the alcohol she'd drunk which loosened her tongue and made her say aloud something she'd only felt deep inside. 'And somehow it seemed right that our bodies should do what our souls had already done.'

Instantly regretting the awkwardly phrased, emotionally charged words, and expecting a scornful response, she braced herself, but he sat without moving a muscle, his face set into a bronze mask.

After a taut silence, he asked abruptly, 'When did you first meet your ex-fiancé?'

Thrown by the sudden change of subject, she blinked and stammered, 'A-about nine months ago.'

'Were there any other men in your life before him that I didn't get to know about?'

'No.'

'Why? You were a beautiful and very desirable young woman.'

Flushing, aware that the words were an indictment rather than a compliment, she said sharply, 'I don't know why. There just weren't.'

But she did know why. After the trauma of her eighteenth birthday, and the dreadful days that had followed, all her normal warmth, her natural feelings and reactions, had been frozen, entombed beneath a glacial despair.

Trying to put the past behind her and rebuild her life,

she'd concentrated on her work and music, withdrawing into her shell if any man so much as looked at her.

Saul lifted a dark brow, 'So what did Mallard have that made him so special?'

'Determination,' she said, with a wry touch of humour. And by that time she'd been almost ready to try out a new relationship. She had been lonely and, not at heart a career-woman, wanted a husband and children before it was too late.

'So when did you begin to sleep with him?'

She was flustered. 'I—I don't remember exactly. Does it matter?'

'Oh, yes, it matters. And surely that's not the kind of thing any woman would forget?'

'Well, I... Fairly soon, I suppose.' Rallying a little, she added, 'As I said, he was very sexy.'

Thoughtfully, Saul remarked, 'When we made love just now, if I hadn't known you weren't, I would have sworn you were still a virgin.'

Watching the colour flood into her face, he went on smoothly, 'Mallard might have been as sexy as hell, but I find it very hard to believe that you and he were ever lovers.'

'Why should I have said we were if we weren't?'

'Why, indeed? Unless it was to hide the fact that your only sexual experience had been the somewhat traumatic one you shared with me.'

Hands clenched into fists, she fought back. 'You know Richard and I went away together. Your detective told you.'

'He also told me that Mallard drove back to New York the next day, alone, and that you were left to settle the bill and find your own way home.'

'Did he have the room bugged too?' she asked bitterly.

'If he had, what would he have heard, Autumn?'

At the end of her tether, she cried, 'He would have heard

us quarrelling...' Then, with a kind of dull despair, 'Richard had expected me to—to take precautions. He was furious when he found I hadn't.' Swallowing, she went on, 'He said I'd had no intention of going through with it, that I was a frigid little bitch...'

He'd thrown the accusation at her as though it made her worthless, destroying any last trace of confidence in herself as a woman. 'And that was one of the kinder things he called me... Now are you satisfied?'

'More satisfied than he was, apparently. I take it you had intended to sleep with him?'

'Yes,' she admitted wearily. 'He'd been pressing me to for a long time, but somehow I couldn't. I guess I was scared... He must have thought I was holding out until I had a wedding-ring on my finger, because he suggested bringing our wedding-date forward. But I knew I couldn't marry him until I was sure I wasn't... Until I was sure I *could* respond to him. I wanted a warm, loving relationship...'

'And did you?'

'Did I what?'

'Love him.'

'He was very attractive and I liked him a lot.'

'Is that all?' Saul made no attempt to hide his derision.

With a wry smile, she said, 'Don't knock it. It seemed to be a breakthrough, a good start. After more than three years of being alone...'

Only she hadn't been alone. Though separated for those years, she and Saul had never really been apart; he'd always been there at the back of her head...

Scathingly, he remarked, 'If your feelings for Mallard were so lukewarm, I'm surprised you agreed to marry him.'

'I was fed up with living alone in a furnished apartment. I thought I was ready to make a real home, to have a husband and children. But when it came to the crunch...'

She rubbed a hand over her eyes as if trying to wipe away a disturbing memory. 'Perhaps I'm not cut out to be a wife and mother.'

'Don't talk such rubbish,' he said roughly. 'One disastrous experience might have put you off sex for a while, but you're certainly not frigid. I've just proved that to you.'

Getting to his feet, he slid one arm behind her back and the other under her knees and lifted her high in his arms. 'Now come to bed and let me prove it all over again.'

Those cool, intelligent grey eyes were fixed on her face, curious, watchful, calculating the effect of what he'd just said.

She made no protest, partly because she knew it would fall on deaf ears, and partly because she was choked by a kind of sick excitement.

But *could* he again? So soon?

As though reading her thoughts, he grinned briefly. 'Celibacy doesn't come easy to me, and for a long time circumstances have forced me to be celibate. Now, to paraphrase a distinguished poet, I find myself with not only the maximum temptation, but the maximum opportunity to indulge myself.'

Outside the parlour, which was still partially lit by the dying fire, it seemed pitch-black. Shakily, Autumn suggested, 'Don't you think we should have a lamp?'

'There's no need. I'm quite used to making my way in the dark,' Saul answered, as he crossed the hall and mounted the stairs with complete confidence. Smoothly he added, 'Thanks to you, I've had a lot of practice.'

She winced at the intentional cruelty.

Without warning he set her on her feet, steadying her when she swayed. 'Wait here a minute.'

Standing in the darkness, her heart thumping, Autumn was utterly disorientated; it seemed an age before she heard the floorboard creak, and then the scrape of a match.

A moment later yellow lamplight illuminated the bare
landing and she realised she was standing just outside the
bathroom door.

'Take this with you—' he handed her the lamp '—while
I go and settle Beth down for the night. When I get back
I'll expect to find you in bed.' Then, as though to eliminate
any possible doubt, '*My* bed.'

Like a robot she cleaned her teeth, then, having taken
off her dressing-gown and nightdress and unwound the
crêpe bandage, stepped under the shower.

Disregarding the vagaries of the pump, she stood for a
long time letting the hot water cascade over her while steam
rose in clouds, swirling like smoke in the lamplight.

While her mind seemed dazed, stupefied, her body felt
sleek, satisfied, somehow different, as though it had finally
come alive in the fullest sense of the word.

Someone had once described love as the gift of life. Perhaps lovers gave each other life. Maybe that was what, for
the vast majority of people, made having someone to love
so irresistible, so *necessary*.

As soon as she turned off the water, cold air wrapped
round her. Shivering, she towelled herself vigorously before
hurriedly getting back into her night-things.

Well aware that if she didn't obey Saul's orders he would
only come and fetch her, she hobbled into his room.

Anxiety, anticipation, and a kind of feverish excitement
mingling, she felt at the same time both weary and wakeful.

Putting the lamp on the bedside cabinet, she saw that her
case and other belongings had been brought up and placed
on a carved chest beneath the window.

The curtains were open and, looking through the latticed
panes, she saw that the snow had stopped falling and the
night was still and tranquil.

Though the sky was moonless, in the snowy light she

could make out the moors stretching away, remote and desolately beautiful, beneath their white blanket.

Outlined against the blackness, a craggy outcrop marked the top of a rise, and beneath the tumbled rocks stretched a narrow plateau of smooth snow. Her imagination peopled it with two dark figures, a man wearing breeches and a woman in a cloak, holding hands…

She gave a little shriek when fingers brushed the back of her neck.

'My, but you are jumpy.' Saul sounded amused.

'No wonder, when you creep up on me like that,' she retorted crossly.

'You were standing so still. What were you thinking about?'

After a moment's hesitation, she pointed. 'See that rocky ridge…?'

'Whinsill Crag.'

'I was just thinking that it's the kind of place where the ghosts of Cathy and Heathcliff might walk.'

Half expecting him to scoff, she was surprised when he asked quite seriously, 'Would you say we could be the modern counterparts of that famous pair?'

'I—I don't understand what you mean,' she stammered. 'What you're getting at.'

'No one could call Cathy and Heathcliff romantic. Emily created savage lovers who wrecked each others' lives, and tore each other apart. Yet she made Cathy say, "Whatever our souls are made of, his and mine are the same…"'

With a touch of wry mockery, he went on, 'Earlier you implied that you once believed our souls were as one…and you may well have been right.'

Unsure whether or not he was joshing, Autumn stood quite still while her green-gold eyes lifted to his face.

'However, at the moment it isn't your soul I'm interested in, just your body. I want you naked on your back beneath me.' The lamplight caught his little twisted smile, and she saw his features were taut with desire.

'On the surface, what I feel is simple male lust, primitive need, elemental hunger, which any woman could assuage…' His voice dropped to a murmur. 'But for some strange reason you are the only woman who will do.'

Suddenly distrusting the ironic note that had crept into his voice, she said, 'Don't you mean I'm the only one available?'

He clicked his tongue at her reprovingly. 'Now you've spoilt the atmosphere.'

'How do you mean?' she asked shortly.

He shrugged. 'I decided if you were in the right emotional frame of mind, and you believed we both thought our relationship had an added dimension, I might get an immediate and passionate response, instead of having to work for a reluctant one.'

'You swine!' she choked.

Laughing at her fury, he queried, 'Can you make it to the bed or shall I carry you?'

'Keep your hands off me,' she choked, bitterly hurt and angry that he'd taken her deepest feelings and mocked and ridiculed them.

Head high, she stalked to the bed and, taking off her dressing-gown, was about to climb in when, indicating her nightdress, he said trenchantly, 'You won't be needing that.'

Tight-lipped, she discarded it.

This time, she swore, no matter what he did to her, the only response he was going to get was cold indifference.

Against her bare skin the bed felt like the icy wastes of Antarctica, so the cold part should be easy, she thought with a bitter quirk of humour, assiduously looking the other way while he swiftly stripped off his clothes.

But it was when he got in beside her and drew her close against his warm, strong body, that once again she began to shiver.

CHAPTER EIGHT

NEXT morning, when Autumn stirred and opened her eyes, thin gleams of watery sunlight were fingering the room.

A quick, wary glance confirmed what she'd already been sure of; she was alone in the high, old-fashioned bed.

It had been almost dawn before she'd fallen asleep, having lain for hours listening to Saul's quiet, even breathing.

Her body spent, her weary mind had refused to rest, churning out jumbled thoughts and images like a malfunctioning video she was unable to switch off.

Now, with the return of consciousness, it started again, memory re-running the tape, making her relive every second of the time spent in his arms.

Knowing she couldn't deflect him from his purpose, and determined not to give him the satisfaction of a response, she had stoked the fires of anger and resentment and for a short while managed to remain outwardly unmoved.

With nothing but his own desire to satisfy, she had hoped he would lose patience fairly quickly and just take her, but murmuring mockingly, 'It will be interesting to see how long you can keep it up,' he had laid siege.

Showing himself even more determined than she was, he had set to with leisurely thoroughness to use all his seductive skill and expertise to coax a response from her rigid body.

Whispering how beautiful she was, how desirable, how infinitely pleasurable he found it to have her in his bed, in his arms, he had fondled her with obvious enjoyment.

His lips against the warm hollow at the base of her throat, he had murmured, 'I've been deprived of my sight for so long that I'd like to throw back the duvet and see my opal lying just above your breasts, watch your body react to the touch of my hands...'

Feeling her shiver, he had added regretfully, 'But the air's too chilly, so I'll just have to imagine how your nipples would look dusky-pink and velvety and your skin glow golden as honey in the lamplight.'

In spite of all her attempts to the contrary, the erotic words and his unhurried, passionate caresses began to melt the ice she had surrounded herself with, causing an insidious warmth, making her body quiver into life and play the traitor to her will.

And of course he knew.

Though she lay with her eyes shut tightly and her teeth clenched together, it was impossible to hide the racing pulse, the taut nipples, and the liquid heat which his remorseless hands engendered as they touched and stroked and explored.

Expecting swift, triumphant possession, she was surprised when he began to kiss her gently, tantalisingly, brushing her closed lips with the tip of his tongue, making her long to open her mouth and respond with sweet passion...

Suddenly assailed by a mixture of self-reproach and humiliation, she jerked her head away and, opening her eyes, stared up at him stonily.

A muscle flicked by his hard, beautiful mouth. Sighing, he instructed, 'Stop fighting me, Autumn, and kiss me back. You know you want to. You're deliberately suppressing your own feelings and—'

'I don't want to kiss you back.' She spat out the lie. 'I have no feelings for you. All I want is that you should get on with it. Satisfy yourself and then leave me alone.'

She heard the sharp hiss of his breath before, his hands gripping her shoulders, he muttered, 'When you say things like that it makes you sound little better than a whore.'

Coldly, she said, 'But that's all I am. That's what you've made me. Except that I'm using my body not to earn money but to pay off a debt.'

Fury flashed in his silvery eyes.

For an instant she thought he was going to strike her and instinctively flinched away from the expected blow.

It didn't come. Despite the wilful provocation, his self-control held good.

In a queer twisted way she would have welcomed it if he had struck her. She *wanted* to hate him, and a blow would have provided further justification.

'Very well...' His voice sounded icily composed. 'If you're determined to act like a whore, then that's how I'll treat you...'

A cruel hand took her chin and forced her head round. Looking up into a dark face from which all emotion had been wiped save lust, she shuddered. 'There's one good thing about a whore,' he added with silky contempt, 'she's always available.'

His body effortlessly dominating hers, he took her with a fierce, primitive passion, arousing an answering passion which swept her along like a tidal wave, leaving her spent and quivering in his arms.

Stroking a hand lightly down her smooth cheek and throat, he taunted, 'Try telling me you didn't enjoy that, my love.'

'Don't call me your love,' she flared. 'Don't *ever* call me that.' She couldn't bear it.

A white line appeared round his mouth and the hand lying on her throat tightened a little. When she swallowed convulsively, he said with dangerous softness, '*I* give the orders around here. Don't ever forget that, my love.'

There was a taut silence, then, reaching to turn off the lamp, he informed her with cold disdain, 'I've had enough of you for one night. You can go to sleep now.'

But it was he who had slept while she had lain wide awake, confused and agitated thoughts milling about in her head.

So much had happened since her visit to Mr Baber's office, shock following on shock so rapidly that her mind felt jarred, incapable of coherent thought.

But amid all the turmoil, the conflicting emotions, one thing she could be truly happy and thankful for was that he had finally regained his sight. That in itself was so wonderful it made everything else bearable.

Holding on to that thought like a lifeline, Autumn got out of bed, not yet ready to face the coming day, but knowing she must.

She was relieved to find that her ankle was no longer swollen and, if she moved with care, only slightly painful.

Beyond the beck the moors stretched away, cold and bleak beneath their blanket of white, but drops of water were dripping from the eaves and running down the diamond-leaded panes, indicating a thaw.

As she looked through the casement a movement caught her eye. Saul, Beth by his side, was returning from an early-morning walk. He was bare-headed, but wearing his tinted glasses against the snow-glare.

Man and dog had started to cross the bridge when Saul glanced up and saw her. He lifted his hand in an ironic salute.

Oddly flustered, she turned away and, as the chilly air goose-fleshed her bare skin, reached hurriedly for her fleecy robe which had been hung behind the door.

A hot, refreshing shower took away some of her stiffness and soothed the slight aches and pains, the tenderness, which had resulted from Saul's passionate lovemaking.

When she'd dried herself, rubbing a head which felt curiously light, she put on clean undies, a wool skirt patterned in shades of brown, gold and burnt ochre, and a fine, oatmeal-coloured shirt-blouse.

Not wanting to face Saul with dark shadows beneath her eyes and a tell-tale pallor, she put on some make-up, applying a rosy blusher to her cheeks.

Somehow it only served to emphasise her paleness.

Thinking with dissatisfaction that the spiky hair and the coins of colour made her look a cross between a pathetic clown and some French waif, she scrubbed most of it off with a tissue, and, having tried unsuccessfully to flatten her hair, felt a pang of regret for her ill-considered action.

Telling herself sternly that it was much too late for regrets, she went downstairs, an outward composure belying the inner turmoil.

Beth greeted her at the kitchen door, plume of a tail waving, and enjoyed a fondle before returning to her place by the fire.

His dark hair slightly dishevelled, as though he hadn't found time to comb it since his walk, Saul was standing by the stove cooking breakfast while he listened to the radio.

He was wearing olive-green trousers and a close-fitting black sweater which threw his facial bone-structure into sharp relief and added to the impact of that lean, devilishly handsome face.

Switching off the radio, he asked pleasantly, 'How is your ankle this morning?'

'It's fine.' Though she tried to echo his agreeable tone, even in her own ears her voice sounded stilted.

'Bacon and egg suit you?' Without waiting for an answer, he congratulated, 'Your timing is impeccable. Sit down, it's just about ready.'

'Thank you, but I'm not—'

'Autumn...' he said warningly.

He had discarded his glasses, and seeing the chilling determination in his grey eyes she sat down and, without further protest, accepted the plate he set in front of her.

By the time she'd forced down the first couple of mouthfuls her appetite had stirred into life.

Hungry now, she would have found the rest of the meal comparatively easy to cope with if, while they ate, he hadn't watched her with a penetrating scrutiny that made her feel like some specimen under a microscope and made her want to squirm.

When both plates were empty, he reached for the coffeepot and filled their cups, remarking casually, 'As soon as we've finished our coffee I'd like you to pack so we can get off.'

'Get off?' she echoed. 'You mean leave here?'

'Yes.'

Shock loosening her tongue, she blurted out, 'But I thought you intended to stay at Farthing Beck until your book was finished?'

'I did. However, my plans have changed.' Carelessly, he added, 'I can write it just as well at home.'

Trying to lasso her scattered wits, she asked, 'But why go so suddenly?'

'Despite a temporary thaw, the Met. Office forecast for this area is for heavy and prolonged snow. Having no desire to be trapped here, maybe for several weeks, I'd like to get away before the weather worsens.'

'Oh,' she said hollowly.

His eyes on her face, he raised a dark, winged brow. 'Anyone would think you didn't want to go.'

Somehow she gathered herself, and scoffed, 'Now, surely you know better than that?'

But even as she spoke she realised that he was right. Her palms clammy, her heart thudding against her ribs, she observed as levelly as possible, 'You said your plans have changed... In what way?'

He answered obliquely, 'Though you agreed to...shall we say, pay your debt, I'm not happy with things as they are.'

'Then you intend to let me go?'

Eyes glinting, he advised her mockingly, 'Precisely the opposite. I intend to alter your status. Tie you to me more closely.'

Her beautiful heart-shaped face pale and tense, she stared at him while her labouring brain struggled to take in all the implications. 'Surely you don't mean...?'

'Joanna was going to be my wife. I told you last night that I intended you to take her place. The only thing that's changed is the timing.'

Smoothly, he went on, 'I had thought we'd marry in the new year, after my book was finished. But your remarks last night have made me revise that decision. Rather than having a reluctant whore in my bed, I want a willing wife...and soon.'

To be his wife was what she'd always wanted. Her dream come true. But not like this. Not hating and despising her. Not just to gratify an obsession. Not for revenge...

'No,' she whispered, white to the lips.

As though she hadn't spoken, he went on, 'But that isn't the only reason for haste. When I first brought you here I presumed that in this day and age a woman of twenty-two would have had some sexual experience, and would almost certainly be protected...'

Painful colour flooded into her face, but she kept her head high.

'As I was wrong on both counts, and there's a chance that you might already be pregnant, it presents an even more pressing reason to get married without delay...'

Oh, but it would be wonderful to be with him on a permanent basis, his companion by day and his lover by night. To lie in his arms and find passion and excitement and sweet ecstasy there…

But knowing he didn't love her would make the aftertaste as bitter as gall.

Huskily, she said, 'I don't want to be your wife.'

'Afraid it would mean emotional involvement? Scared you'd have to make a commitment?'

Leaning forward, his brilliant eyes on her face, he probed, 'Didn't you once dream of marrying me? Dream of us living together happily ever after?'

She winced, his words painful as a scalpel opening up an old wound. 'That was a long time ago.'

'Do dreams ever die?'

'I don't want to be your wife,' she repeated through stiff lips.

'Ah, but it's what *I* want that counts.'

She couldn't bear it. She couldn't!

Jumping up so clumsily that her chair toppled over, she backed away until she was brought up short by the draining-board.

He got to his feet and came to loom over her, looking down into her flushed face.

'You can't make me marry you,' she whispered through a dry throat.

'That's quite true.' His hands slid up her arms and came to rest with his thumbs pressing against her breasts, sending a jolt of electricity through her. 'But if you look at it logically I'm sure you'll see it's for the best.'

'How can it be for the best when we hate each other?' she choked.

'*Do* you hate me, Autumn?'

She wanted to cry yes, but she couldn't bring herself to tell such a monstrous lie. Mutely she shook her head.

'Then there's hope for us yet,' he said sardonically.

'Once you've stopped fighting me and learnt how to be an amenable little wife, though our marriage may not come up to your girlish expectations, I dare say we'll get along well enough.'

A surge of pain closed her eyes, and a giant fist seemed to tighten around her heart. With calculated cruelty he'd mocked her, taken her precious dreams and trampled them underfoot.

'Don't look so stricken.' There was a razor-sharp edge to his voice. 'When you get used to the idea you'll find there are plenty of things in its favour. Plenty of reasons why it should succeed.'

Gathering the tattered shreds of her pride around her like a defensive cloak, she looked him in the face and said coolly, 'Funny, but I can't think of one.'

'Then I'll list them for you,' he told her crisply. 'You want a husband and a family, you've admitted that, but what happened when you were eighteen has given you a complex. Made you scared of men, scared of sex, of being frigid...

'Well, I've proved that as far as we are concerned there's no real problem. Even when your will is fighting me I can get your body to respond.

'As for me, I've lost any taste I might have had for casual affairs. I want a permanent relationship, the same woman in my bed each night. You.'

'It would never work,' she cried desperately. 'You told me that all you wanted was sex, to—to sate yourself with me.'

'Not *all*. I want an attractive wife—what man wouldn't?—yet no matter how beautiful she was or how good in bed, a woman who was shallow and empty-headed would soon bore me to tears—'

Recalling past bitterness, she broke in, 'You're forgetting one thing. I'm not in your class and never will be.'

'Class be damned,' he said shortly. 'You've got brains as well as beauty, you're gifted and intelligent, you have depth and intrinsic worth as well as a sense of humour…'

She gave him a look that clearly indicated he was wasting his breath.

'And when you get through being defiant you'll admit that we have a lot in common, we share the same interests, and we were good friends once…'

We were good friends once…

But that Saul had been a different man. Though in many ways tough and formidable, with her he'd always—or at least until Joanna came along—proved to be kind, considerate, and even-tempered…nothing like this ruthless, hard-eyed stranger.

'We could be again. Don't you think so, Autumn?'

Having admitted that he couldn't force her to marry him, he seemed to be taking a great deal of trouble to persuade her, she thought, suddenly afraid of weakening. If she agreed, she would be leaving herself wide open to pain, living with the knowledge that he didn't love her…

But he was going on. 'As well as a wife to warm my bed, I want a stimulating companion, someone to enjoy day-to-day living with…'

'Don't you mean a whipping-boy?' she asked tautly. 'Someone to punish for your past suffering? Someone to vent your present bitterness on?'

His hands tightened until she winced, then, as though making a great effort at self-control, he slackened his grip and let her go.

'No, I don't mean a whipping-boy,' he said evenly. 'I'm prepared to try and look forward, not back…and, mixed with a liberal amount of honey, bitterness can be turned into sweetness.'

She was torn. If only he meant it. If only they could both

put the past behind them… Thinking aloud, she whispered, 'It would be taking a terrible risk.'

'I've no intention of letting you go, so it's a risk you're going to have to take…and it's largely in your own hands.'

A shade drily, she queried, 'You mean it's up to me to provide the honey?'

Showing healthy white teeth in a mocking smile, he said, 'That's exactly what I mean… Now, if you'll tidy away the breakfast things, I'll pack the cases and bring them down.'

He seemed to have taken it for granted that the matter was settled.

Unable, at that moment, to fight any more, not even sure if she wanted to, Autumn set about clearing the table.

Some half an hour later, when they were ready to leave, Saul opened the front door, and she found that the weather forecast had been accurate. Already the sun had gone from a sky of icy pearl and the air held a chill bleakness which suggested the overnight thaw was already over and more snow was imminent.

Like the result of some conjuring trick, his Rover was standing exactly where it had been before it vanished. Watching him toss their cases into the boot, though it no longer seemed to matter overmuch, Autumn was moved to ask, 'Where did you put it?'

'Round the back in one of the old barns.'

'I'm surprised I didn't hear the engine.'

'The house has comparatively small windows and the thick walls deaden sound,' he answered prosaically.

Seeing he'd replaced his glasses, and unsure whether they were suitable for driving, she asked, 'Do you want me to take the wheel?'

She was relieved when he shook his head. 'You look tired, and until we get further south conditions are bound to be tricky.'

He helped her into the front passenger seat and got in beside her. A few seconds later, a little frown of concentration between his dark brows, he was coaxing the car over the slippery cobbles and across the hump-backed bridge.

As they turned down the track towards Feldon, glancing back at the grey stone house, Autumn experienced nothing but a strange emptiness.

So much had happened there that she knew she ought to feel something on leaving it—regret, relief, *something*... But over the past forty-eight hours she'd run through the gamut of emotions, and for the present she was totally drained.

When they reached the Green Man, Saul drew up outside, remarking, 'Won't be a minute. I'm just going to let the Skiptons know we're leaving, and give my housekeeper a call to tell her what time we expect to be home.'

Before getting out, he removed the keys from the ignition and, slanting a glance at her, said with brittle humour, 'I don't want to put ideas into your head.'

'You don't need to,' she retorted, and saw his face darken.

But, watching his tall figure disappear round the side of the pub, she admitted to herself that, even if he'd left the keys, she wouldn't, couldn't, have driven away without him.

Stunned, off-balance, her mind suspended in a kind of limbo, she could only wait until she'd recovered both her mental and emotional equilibrium before deciding whether to make a run for it or take a chance on marriage.

Saul was back quite quickly, his feet scrunching on the rapidly freezing slush. Taking his seat behind the wheel without a word and with barely a glance, he drove the few yards to the single petrol pump and had the car filled up before starting homeward.

It was a slow journey, and long before they had left the

snow behind them and were running into better weather, Autumn was fast asleep.

Apart from a short lunchtime stop at a Midlands pub for coffee and sandwiches which, dazed and disorientated, she ate like a somnambulist, she slept all the way.

Her name being repeated disturbed her. Opening heavy eyes, she sat up to find they were in Godsend, on Riverside Drive, the quiet, residential road which ran by the Thames.

This far south it was dry and bright, the late afternoon sun gilding the water and edging with gold the drifts of brown leaves still lying beneath the skeletal trees.

Making an attempt to pull herself together, she mumbled, 'Then you still live at The Rowans.'

It had been a statement rather than a question, and she was taken by surprise when he answered shortly, 'No,' and, turning into a well-known drive, stopped in front of the black and white half-timbered cottage.

When Saul came round and put a hand beneath her elbow, Autumn got out of the car as though in a dream. A moment later he had opened the studded oak door and was ushering her into a panelled hall.

Seeming to be held in a kind of time-warp, Cecilia Cottage was just as she remembered it. It even smelt the same, a nostalgic combination of beeswax and lavender and the sharper scent of pine.

Wandering through the picturesque, low-ceilinged rooms, a familiar ghost revisiting past haunts, she saw that even the antique furniture, with its softly glowing patina of age, was the same. The bow-fronted sideboard, the grandfather clock, the rosewood piano...

Logs and pine-cones had been piled in the stone fireplaces and bowls of bronze chrysanthemums glowed against the dark panelling.

No fires were lit, but the air was comfortably warm, and

the old place had the contented feel of a house that was well-loved and cared for.

Apart from an *en suite* bathroom added to the master bedroom, upstairs too was unaltered. Her own room had the same cottage-garden curtains, the same faded, yet still beautiful rugs, the same narrow white bed that she'd slept in as a child.

How many times had she lain in that bed and, both sleeping and awake, dreamt of Saul? Dreamt of the time he'd tell her they belonged together and ask her to be his wife…dreamt of bearing his children and spending the rest of her life just loving him. Loving him…

Moons away, caught up in the past, she became aware that he was standing silently in the gathering dusk, watching her.

Seventeen again, filled with the purest, sweetest emotion, she looked at him with huge, dazed eyes, and said his name softly, wonderingly, a query in her voice.

As though in response he came up close, his thickly lashed, silvery eyes on her face.

Like someone in a trance she put out a hand and touched his cheek, feeling the slight roughness beneath her palm.

When he continued to stand quite still, she traced the outline of his beautifully chiselled lips with her fingertips then, as if impelled, put her hands flat against his chest and stood on tiptoe to touch her mouth to his, the contact warm and light and curiously innocent.

Beneath her palms she felt his heart pick up and begin to race. His arms went round her, pressing her against him, and the kiss took fire.

One of his hands moved down her slender curves, closing over hip and buttock, while the other cupped the back of her head, supporting it against the increasingly passionate demand of his mouth.

Answering that demand, she gave him kiss for kiss with

complete abandon, meeting and matching his passion with a hunger that was at once fierce and tender, sending them both up in flames.

His hands suddenly urgent, he stripped off first her clothes and then his own, and when, having lifted her on to the narrow bed, he joined her there, naked flesh against naked flesh, she felt only an overwhelming gladness.

Lost in a sensual world of wonder and delight, she touched him as she'd always wanted to touch him, stroking his smooth shoulders and the strong column of his throat, caressing the warmth of his nape, running her fingers into his thick dark hair.

Eyes closed, absorbed in the sheer pleasure it was giving her, she explored further, finding the powerful chest muscles, feeling the sprinkle of crisp body-hair beneath her fingertips, following his ribcage down to lean hips and a firm abdomen, glorying in his potent maleness.

She felt his body clench at her light touch and knew a heady sense of power as she squeezed and fondled.

He allowed her to have the initiative and play for a while, then, his own hands and mouth busy, he took control again.

When it finally came, their union was an ecstatic explosion of heat and light, a magical, mystical conflagration, two separate beings joining on all levels to make one shining whole.

This time, when the elation, the euphoria faded, in its aftermath came a quiet peace. A peace that lingered when, instead of leaving her, Saul pulled the covers over them and remained by her side, loose-limbed and relaxed.

He offered no tender words, no lover's embrace, but, only too grateful that he was *there*, she felt his warmth and listened to his light, even breathing until she fell asleep.

CHAPTER NINE

WHEN, still half asleep, Autumn opened her eyes, it was dark and she was alone in the narrow bed. Immediately she was overwhelmed by a kind of sick panic, convinced that Saul had gone forever and she would never see him again.

Her heart racing, her breath coming in ragged gasps, she sat bolt upright.

It was a few seconds before she was able to push the waking nightmare away and make a positive effort to calm her agitation.

Gradually her heartbeat slowed, her breathing eased, and common sense reasserted itself.

She was just wondering what time it was when the door opened, spilling a rectangle of light from the landing.

'So you're awake.' Saul walked in, carrying a cup of tea. He was wearing grey trousers and a striped shirt open at the neck, the sleeves rolled up to his elbows.

'It's almost eight o'clock—' he answered her unspoken question as he stooped to switch on the bedside lamp '—and dinner's ready.'

Putting her tea down on the cabinet, he sat on the edge of her bed.

Becoming aware that she was naked, in sudden embarrassment she tried to pull the covers higher.

'Shy?' he queried with a hint of mockery. 'Surely not?'

Suddenly recalling her earlier uninhibited behaviour, she felt the same kind of shame she'd felt after her eighteenth birthday.

Scalding colour pouring into her face and throat, she bent her head.

He cursed softly, expressively, and a cool hand forced her chin up.

Sounding annoyed, impatient, he said, 'Don't look like that. There's absolutely no need to feel ashamed. Nothing that's happened between us is wrong or degrading...' His hands gripping her shoulders, he shook her slightly. 'You do believe that, don't you?'

She believed there should be no shame in happy, joyful sex between two people who cared about each other. But Saul *didn't* care about her, and the memory of her own shameful behaviour all those years ago, the fear of repeating it, had thrown up a stumbling-block...

When she failed to answer, he sighed. 'You won't feel that way when you're my wife.' Then, seriously, 'I was intending to wait until we were married—' his lips twisted with wry self-mockery '—but I'm only human... Now, come on, drink your tea. And no regrets. It was fantastic...'

His last comment was spreading a healing balm when, rising to his feet, he added trenchantly, 'A bit more practice and Joanna will have nothing on you.'

Watching her flinch, he smiled mirthlessly, then said with easy authority, 'The meal's waiting. Don't be long.'

Watching his broad back disappear through the door, Autumn, though not usually a violent person, felt a fierce desire to throw the tea at him.

Instead, her hand shaking, she picked it up carefully and drank it.

His words, 'until we were married,' danced in her mind... But if the breathtaking experience they'd shared had moved him so little that he could still taunt her about Joanna, what chance had any marriage got?

Though if Saul's barbs reached their mark, wasn't it her

own fault? She shouldn't allow herself to be so wide-open, so easily wounded.

She was no longer a foolish, vulnerable girl, so why behave like one? A woman now, she had hard-won reserves of inward strength and outward composure.

The years spent in New York had helped to toughen her, given her some degree of self-confidence, a surface gloss that had scarcely been scratched until that disastrous weekend with Richard.

Even that had been swiftly varnished over until, faced with the prospect of seeing Saul once more, she'd instantly gone to pieces.

But surely, after all that had happened, the worst of the trauma was behind her? Now it was time to pull herself together and put that smooth, impenetrable armour back in place.

Getting out of bed, she ignored the voice that scoffed, Fat chance! and told herself firmly that she would at least *pretend* to be cool and impervious.

If she was able to convince Saul that he could no longer hurt her, he might stop trying.

Her clothes, she found, had been collected and hung neatly over a chair, and her case and other belongings had been placed on a blanket-chest.

Though an intensely masculine man, and in no way pernickety, Saul had a liking for order.

He also had a liking for giving orders and having them obeyed, she reminded herself with dry humour, and he'd said, 'Don't be long'.

But, refusing to hurry, she found her wash-bag and made a leisurely toilet before making her way downstairs, her head high, her face cool and composed.

As she passed the kitchen door, Beth, ears pricked, looked up from her place in front of the Aga and waved her plume of a tail by way of greeting.

In the adjoining dining-room Saul had just placed a casserole dish on the table and was wearing an oven mitt patterned like a crocodile with gaping jaws.

'Very macho,' Autumn commented with deliberate sarcasm.

Pulling out a chair for her, he grinned, unruffled. 'Mrs Hawkins chose it especially.'

Her heart turning over in her breast at that sudden, almost boyish smile, Autumn managed to say casually, 'Then she's still with you?'

Maggie Hawkins, hard-working and cheerful, had been his parents' housekeeper, and after their deaths had stayed on to look after him.

'Oh, yes.' He helped Autumn to a generous amount of chicken and vegetables. 'When I bought this place, she and her husband moved from their terraced house into The Rowans. Bob Hawkins has been an invalid for years, so a bungalow right next door was ideal, especially as George lodges with them and lends them a hand.'

'George acted as your chauffeur?'

'And my secretary. Though it really wasn't his cup of tea, he proved invaluable while I was blind. He's semi-retired now, though he lends Bob a hand and takes care of both gardens.'

An odd lump in her throat, Autumn asked, 'Why did you buy Cecilia Cottage?'

His expression guarded, Saul shrugged. 'I'd always liked it.'

'How long have you lived here?'

'I moved in as soon as I came out of hospital. It stood empty after you and your parents left. The old lady who owned it was planning to go abroad and didn't want to re-let it, so I bought the place, lock, stock and barrel.'

A trifle unevenly, she remarked, 'And you haven't changed a thing.'

'Apart from putting in a second bathroom and some un-obtrusive central heating.'

'A great improvement,' she admitted.

With no change of tone, he asked, 'Then you'll be quite content to live here when we're married?'

Suddenly the ball was in her court and she had no idea how to play it.

Ducking the bigger issue in favour of the smaller one, she answered his question with a question of her own. 'If I said I didn't want to live here, what would you do?'

'As I've always considered that it's the woman who makes the home, I'd allow you a free hand to choose some-where else... within certain limits, that is.'

'Oh...' She failed to hide her surprise.

'I regard marriage as a partnership. Or were you ex-pecting complete subjugation?' he queried sardonically.

Without having thought about it in depth, as things were, that *was* what she'd been expecting.

'Not exactly,' she lied, 'but I...'

'Would feel a lot more confident if you could change me back into the man I was?'

It was so close to what she'd been thinking that she flushed uncomfortably. 'As I'm largely responsible for you being as you are now, I have no right to—'

Levelly, he broke in, 'You have any rights you care to claim... So, do you want to start looking for another house?' Once again the important question was disguised by the lesser one.

Looking up, she met grey eyes gone dark and smoky and saw he was waiting for her reply with fixed intensity. For whatever reason, it *mattered* to him.

She remembered his words: 'I'm prepared to try and look forward, not back...and, mixed with a liberal amount of honey, bitterness can be turned into sweetness...'

He was willing to do his best, and in return she could

give him the sweetness of love. It would be her secret gift to him, and maybe in time it might help to turn his bitter animosity if not into love, then at least into liking and forgiveness.

If they were ever able to recapture their old happy companionship it would be all that, and more than, she dared hope for.

'Well, do you?' He was growing impatient.

Steadily, she answered, 'No, I'll be quite content to live here.'

Some powerful emotion crossed his face, but, before she could decipher what it was, it had gone, replaced by a bland mask of indifference.

They were at the coffee stage before he spoke again, then, his voice markedly casual, he asked, 'Would you like a church wedding or a civil ceremony?'

'Do *you* have any preference?'

'I do,' he admitted. Then he added smoothly but inexorably, 'However, in the circumstances, I'd like you to decide.'

They were talking as though they were polite strangers, she thought in dismay, not like two people who were intending to spend the rest of their lives together.

His handsome, thickly lashed eyes held a watchful, waiting look, but she was unable to tell what answer he was hoping for.

Would he 'in the circumstances' prefer a short, businesslike civil ceremony? Well, if he would he should have said so, she thought, and announced firmly, 'I'd like to get married in St Thomas's Church.'

'Then I'll see about getting a special licence.' If he was put out by her answer, he hid it well.

After a moment, his face expressionless, he asked casually, 'More coffee?'

'No, thanks.' She rose to clear the table, needing something to occupy her.

'Leave it,' he instructed, getting to his feet. 'Mrs Hawkins will see to everything in the morning.'

Hands falling to her sides, Autumn hovered a little helplessly until, with ironic courtesy, he ushered her through to the living-room, where earlier he'd put a match to the fire.

A long, low-beamed room, it looked homely and attractive, with twin standard-lamps shedding pools of light, the logs blazing merrily, and chintz curtains shutting out the November night.

When she took a seat by the fire, he dropped into a chair opposite and regarded her steadily.

In the past, the time they had spent together had always been relaxed and happy, their talk stimulating, their silences comfortable. Now, in spite of the cosy room, there was discomfort, a feeling of tension. Sexual tension.

Restless, on edge, she wondered how on earth they were going to get through the rest of the evening.

Divining her thoughts with unnerving accuracy, he suggested ironically, 'We could always watch television...'

Neither had ever liked television, preferring reading, music, chess, or just talking.

'Unless you'd care to play for me?'

Silently she shook her head. She didn't want to play for him tonight. It was too emotive. Too revealing. Like baring her soul.

'No?' His grey eyes glinted. 'Then what about an early night?'

'I—I'm not tired yet,' she stammered, taken unawares.

'That's good.' He smiled wolfishly. 'I wasn't thinking of sleeping.'

Watching her grow pink and flustered, he stretched out a hand and said softly, 'Come here.'

As though under a spell, she got up and put her hand into his, allowing him to pull her down on his knee.

She'd never sat on his lap before. Not once. Now she was overwhelmed by diverse and exciting sensations. She could hear the quickening beat of his heart and, beneath her buttocks, feel his firm flesh, solid bone and muscle. His breath was fresh and sweet against her lips and, too close to focus on, his grey eyes were a silvery blur.

One hand resting just below her breast, he dipped his head and touched his mouth to the side of her neck in a sensuous caress.

Taking a shaky breath, she wondered how it was that he could heat her blood and make every nerve-ending sing into life with just the lightest touch.

She had always loved him, but never expected the vibrant carnality that had flared into life between them. Picturing in her girlish daydreams a gentle, contented, almost passionless lovemaking, she had never, ever imagined how fiercely her body would burn for his.

He had lifted his head and was studying her expressive face. When his gaze dropped to her breasts, enticingly outlined by the soft material of her blouse, she shivered, the sensation almost as palpable as a physical touch.

With the pressure of a single finger against her chin, he turned her face to his.

Green-gold eyes wide and dazed, she lifted her hand and touched his jaw, watching her fingertips follow the slight cleft, feeling the rasp of stubble beneath them.

As though there was no help for it, her gaze moved up to his clean-cut mouth and lingered there. Oh, but it was beautiful, the top lip thin and firm, the lower fuller, a turn-on combination of austereness and sensuality.

'Kiss me,' he urged softly. 'You know you want to.'

Though his lips parted seductively beneath hers, he sat quite still and passive, making no move to take the initiative or deepen the kiss. His mouth was like sleek satin in contrast to the roughness of his jaw.

While she kissed him, learning the exciting taste and texture of his lips, without her conscious volition, her hands fumbled to undo the buttons of his shirt, pulling aside the thin cotton to slip inside.

His skin was warm and slightly moist, the sprinkle of dark body-hair crisp beneath her palms.

An involuntary shiver shook her and, her face against his throat now, she swallowed, the ache of anticipation intensifying.

His hands moved to cover her breasts, feeling the rapid rise and fall, the nipples firming beneath that light, sure touch.

Then, more skilful than hers, his fingers dealt with the buttons of her blouse and the front fastening of her bra. Brushing them both aside, he bent his head and began to kiss the creamy, flawless flesh he'd exposed.

'Your skin is so enticing,' he murmured. 'It smells of sun and spring and apple-blossom…'

His lips travelling appreciatively over her warm, soft curves, he continued huskily, 'Your breasts are a delight— firm, shapely, just the right size to fill my hands…and your nipples are perfect, dusky pink and like velvet on my tongue…'

Every erotic word fuelled her libido.

When his hands cupped her breasts and his thumbs began gently to tease the peaks, she gave a strangled gasp.

One hand continued its torment while the other slid up her thigh to find, and slip beneath, the lacy edge of her briefs.

Almost at once she was transfixed, a quivering mass of sensations, held in thrall by those exciting, experienced hands. Hands that tantalised and tormented without satisfying.

While she wondered how long she could endure this agony of expectation, this pleasure that was so exquisite it was almost pain, he kept her delicately poised on the brink, denying her a release, refusing to gratify the need he'd aroused.

Without realising it, she was making little inarticulate sounds in her throat, wordless pleas.

Against her ear, he whispered, 'Talk to me, Autumn…tell me what you want.'

'You know,' she managed hoarsely.

His hands stilled. 'Ah, but I want *you* to tell me. Tell me exactly what I'm doing to you. How I make you feel…'

'I—I…*can't*…'

'Frustrated? Impatient?'

'Yes…impatient…'

'I felt like that for a long time…almost four years. I'd lie awake in the darkness, picturing you naked with my opal lying just above your breasts, aching with frustration…waiting for the day I'd get you back, waiting to make you feel just some of the things I'd felt…'

Like a cold wind, his words dispersed the heated mists of passion, and abruptly the sexual excitement died, leaving her chilled and shivering.

Pushing his hand away, she struggled to her feet, and with shaking fingers pulled her bra together and fastened it, before re-buttoning her blouse.

Watching her through narrowed eyes, he went on mockingly, 'But don't worry, it's no part of my plan to keep you frustrated. Rather, I want you hooked on sex, hopelessly addicted, a devotee who needs the excitement like a drug-taker needs a fix…

'Coming back?' He patted his knee invitingly.

Clenching her teeth against the bitter words that would have betrayed her humiliation, she shook her head. 'I'm going to bed.'

Rising to his feet, he held out his hand. 'Then come to bed with me.'

'I'd rather not,' she refused coolly, adding with derisive politeness, 'Apart from the fact that I've had enough excitement for one day, I should end up despising myself if I were to become ''hopelessly addicted''.'

Grimacing, he said ruefully, 'Hoist with my own petard. Ah, well…'

Though he spoke lightly, she sensed that his regret was genuine, and keen. Intent on arousing her, he'd become aroused himself.

Having put the fireguard in place, he followed her across the hall and up the stairs.

With every step she took she was conscious of his eyes boring into her back, aware of his desire beating against her like a sirocco.

When she would have walked straight past the master bedroom, his hand shot out and encircled her wrist in a steely grip. 'Sure you won't change your mind?'

'Quite sure.'

'I could make you.'

Boldly, she stated, 'I don't believe you'll try.'

'What makes you so sure?'

'Because earlier you said you'd been prepared to wait until we were married.'

'Tonight I seem to be saying a damn sight too much.' He used the hand he was still holding to jerk her into his arms.

She would have pulled away, but he held her there, and said with great deliberation, 'You can hardly refuse me a goodnight kiss.'

Telling herself she would be safe if she kept it brief, she reluctantly lifted her face, and tried not to tremble when he bent to cover her mouth with his.

At first the pressure was light, almost diffident, giving

her a false feeling of safety. Then, softly, seductively, he deepened the kiss until all at once his mouth was ravishing hers and she was lost in a whirlpool of delight.

Body melting, head spinning, she clung to him, never wanting it to end.

Under the fierce onslaught of his lips, she didn't notice that he was once more undoing her blouse. Deftly, without fumbling, he freed the small pearl buttons and slipped his hand inside the soft material to cup her breast.

She felt not only the wild beating of her own heart but the rapid pounding of his, and a movement of his body which betrayed that she had a power over him scarcely less than his over her.

Against her lips, he whispered, 'Of course if you don't *want* to wait…'

If he'd just picked her up and carried her into his bedroom she would have offered little or no resistance. But the whispered words broke the spell.

Somehow she managed to croak, 'I do,' and pulled herself free, staggering as though she were drunk.

She wondered fleetingly if he would try to dissuade her and knew he could do it all too easily.

He made a slight move and she flinched away, exclaiming hoarsely, 'Leave me alone… I don't *want* to sleep with you tonight.'

His face set, the olive skin stretched taut over sharply defined bone-structure, he said with a self-control she was forced to marvel at, 'There's no need to sound so desperate. I told you you had any rights you cared to claim, and that includes the right to say no…only I didn't believe you really wanted to. Goodnight, Autumn. Sleep well.'

Though still relatively inexperienced, she realised that, no matter how controlled he might sound, inwardly he must be struggling to batten down urges which, once aroused, were not easy to suppress.

He disappeared into his room and the door closed behind him with a decisive click, leaving her staring blankly at the panels.

That ironic 'Sleep well' echoing in her ears, she made her way blindly down the landing to her own bedroom.

Moving like an automaton, she rummaged in her case and found a fine lawn nightdress with a demure neckline and short sleeves, before cleaning her teeth in the adjoining bathroom and climbing into bed.

She knew Saul had wanted her badly, so why had he given her the chance to walk away?

Unless he believed she was too much under his spell to take it.

Well, she had confounded him. She had managed to walk away. Not because she didn't want him, she admitted, but because she had been intent on punishing him for what he'd done to her earlier, intent on getting her own back.

And she had succeeded, so why didn't she feel happier about it? More elated?

Because she'd cut off her nose to spite her face. Because she was lying alone in her own narrow bed when she could have been lying in his arms.

Despite everything, she wanted to be with him. It was only her fear of being humiliated further, her pride that had made her walk away.

And what did her pride matter?

Instead of thinking of herself, she should have been thinking of him. Irrespective of what he'd done to her, she *owed* him.

Through her bitter jealousy, her wilful refusal to believe the truth, she had caused him untold physical and mental anguish; caused him to suffer nearly four years of hell, locked away in darkness; caused him to be humiliated, his pride dragged in the dust; caused him to lose both his chosen career and the woman he had loved. Maybe still loved.

It was a damning indictment. And, knowing how much she owed him, she had promised him recompense—herself—by way of compensation.

But when it came to the crunch she hadn't given freely, lovingly. She had been reluctant, afraid of the power he had over her, concerned more about her own pain than his.

In a few days, for better or worse, they would be man and wife. So wasn't it time she put aside her own feelings and considered Saul's?

On a wave of emotion she was out of bed and halfway across the room when an unpalatable thought stopped her in her tracks. If she went to him now she'd been leaving herself wide open to scorn and ridicule...

Coward. It hadn't taken her long to chicken out.

But what if he jeered, taunted her with going just to ease her own frustrations?

So what if he did?

If things were ever going to get any better between them she would have to sink her pride, stop worrying about her own feelings, and start spreading a little of that honey Saul had talked about.

Trying not to think any more, to worry about her reception, she got out of bed and, without switching on the light, padded barefoot along the landing.

At his door, she hesitated, her pride surfacing to fight a rearguard action.

To go in now would mean conceding him victory and offering a complete and abject surrender.

But hadn't some philosopher once said there were times you had to be prepared to lose in order to win?

He might be asleep.

In the circumstances that was unlikely, and if he was she would wake him.

He might reject her.

Biting her lip, she scuttled her pride. That was a chance she would have to take.

Without knocking, she opened the door and walked in.

There was no moon but the sky was clear, and in the semi-darkness she could see he was standing by the window, still fully dressed, looking out over the Thames to the intricate pattern of lights beyond.

Though he must have heard the latch click, he gave not the slightest sign that he knew she was there.

Subduing a craven impulse to turn on her heel and run, she closed the door resolutely behind her and went over to him.

He stood so motionless that he could have been a statue, the gleam of his eyes the only thing about him that seemed alive.

When she was barefoot, her head barely reached his chin. Putting her palms flat against the fine cotton of his unbuttoned shirt, she stood on tiptoe to touch her mouth to his.

For an endless moment Saul remained still and unresponsive, then he stepped back and, showing he understood exactly what she was offering, asked coolly, 'Sure you want to burn your boats?'

Though shaken by his apparent indifference, she answered steadily, 'Quite sure,' and, moving closer, kissed him again.

After what seemed an age his arms went round her and, while relief surged through her, he returned her kiss with a fiery passion that set them both alight.

Lifting her high in his arms he carried her to the bed and laid her down. 'Then we'll make it a glorious blaze.'

And it was glorious, so glorious that she had to clench her teeth to prevent the words of love from pouring out, words of love she was longing to say. But Saul had never believed in her love, she knew, and she couldn't bear it now if he mocked.

* * *

Next morning Autumn awakened slowly, languorously, her world piecing itself together a little at a time. She was aware of a glow of gladness and contentment, a sense of well-being.

Stirring, she found her body nestling against smooth, firm flesh, and her head pillowed in the comfortable junction between chest and shoulder, while the weight of an arm across her back held her securely.

Beneath her cheek was solid bone and muscle and the slight roughness of body-hair. Finest velvet couldn't have felt more wonderful, and happiness lapped round her like a warm tide.

One hand was lying, palm down, on his chest beside her face. Eyes still closed, she flexed her fingers slightly, feeling the sprinkle of short springy hair with pleasure.

Her surrender the previous night had been amply rewarded. Once again he'd proved himself a marvellous lover, exciting, skilful and passionate.

And afterwards, instead of just lifting himself away, he'd rolled over, taking her with him, so that her body had been half supported by his. He had kissed her and held her in his arms, cradling her with an emotion that could have been mistaken for tenderness.

Happier than she'd ever been in her life before, Autumn had fallen asleep with the strong, steady beat of his heart close to her ear.

During those years of physical separation, one of her most piercing regrets had been that she would die without ever having known the delight of falling asleep in his arms and waking with her head on his shoulder.

Now, like some rare and priceless jewel, that gift had been bestowed on her.

Sighing, she tilted her head to glance up at his face and found he was looking down at her, a strange expression in his grey eyes.

Satisfaction? Triumph?

No, the emotion was a great deal more complex than that. She realised with a sudden frisson of alarm that, as well as a kind of anger, it held more than a trace of mingled sadness and despair. It was the look of someone who had longed for the moon and been given merely a beautiful balloon.

As she stared at him that fleeting impression of anger and sadness vanished, to be replaced by an impassive calm that made her wonder if she'd only imagined it.

Dropping a light kiss on her upturned mouth, he hitched them both into a sitting position, and, holding her so that he could look directly into her face, asked, 'Why did you come to me last night, Autumn?'

Because I love you. Because I couldn't see the point of withholding my body when you already have my heart. Because life is too short for us to be apart when we could be together.

No matter what she'd told herself then, the basic reasons were that simple. But they were not reasons she could give him.

Aloud she answered carefully, 'Because I didn't want to go on fighting. In a few days we'll be man and wife, and I...' Put into words at last, the concept was so charged with emotion that she faltered to a stop.

He glanced at her sharply, then, with his face shuttered, giving no clue to his feelings, he said, 'Speaking of which, would you mind a short honeymoon, say ten days? I don't want to postpone starting my book for too long.'

'No, no, of course not. I hadn't expected—' Seeing his sudden scowl, she stopped speaking abruptly.

'A honeymoon?' he asked brusquely. 'Why not? It's quite usual.'

All at once the mood of happiness and contentment was gone, banished as though it had never been.

'Yes, I know,' she agreed uneasily, 'but our marriage is hardly usual… I mean, it's not exactly a—' Once again she broke off.

'A love-match? No, it's hardly that.' His face was set and there was a white line round his mouth. 'But you did say you wanted to be married in church, so I rather presumed you were in favour of keeping up the old traditions.'

'I—I am,' she stammered. 'But, things being as they are, I didn't think you would be.'

Coldly, he said, 'As I only plan to marry once, I fully intend to make the most of it.'

With his free hand he threw back the duvet.

In the long mirror she saw, and was fascinated by, their reflections.

He followed her gaze.

Beneath winged brows, the eyes looking back at her were clear and silvery, beautiful long-lashed eyes in a tough, very masculine face. His jaw darkened with morning stubble and his almost-black hair rumpled into unruly curls, he looked hard and confident and dangerously attractive.

While she had the appearance of a waif, she thought in dismay, her short spiky hair throwing her bone-structure into sharp relief, making her green eyes too big for her face and giving her a haunting, lost look.

Shy, embarrassed, she wanted to turn away from their nakedness, but her eyes were helplessly drawn down.

His olive skin had kept its tan, and beside his well-muscled body she looked pale and deceptively delicate. One strong, dark-fuzzed leg was trapping the slender golden length of hers, and his arm lay, bronzed and muscular, across the soft creaminess of her breasts.

His eyes holding hers through the mirror, with studied insolence he took a pink nipple and rolled it between his finger and thumb, his lips twisting into a cruel little smile when it firmed at his touch.

She sat quite still, letting him do as he wanted, but her face flamed with painful colour. Perhaps it was the contrast between now and the happiness she'd felt earlier that, unexpectedly, made her green eyes fill with tears.

Trying desperately not to, she blinked, and two bright drops spilt over and ran down her cheeks. One of them plopped on to his hand. Mortified, she clumsily wiped it away.

He muttered an oath under his breath and, pulling himself clear, jumped out of bed and headed for the *en suite* bathroom.

At the door he glanced back and, seeing her still sitting there, head bent, said roughly, 'For God's sake don't cry…and have something done about your hair. You look like Little Orphan Annie.'

CHAPTER TEN

As soon as Saul disappeared into the bathroom, Autumn stumbled out of bed and, blinded by tears, fled to her own room. She felt sick and shaken.

As she showered, the hot water failing to stem the flow of tears, she wondered despairingly what had brought about the change in Saul.

On waking, she had believed that things might really work out and happiness might be blossoming. Then, without any warning, the vision of happiness had vanished like some mirage and they were back to arid desert, with Saul setting out to hurt and humiliate her again.

It was almost as if, having expected too much, he'd blamed her for his disappointment. But she'd given him all she had to give, absolute surrender. So what had he wanted that she *hadn't* been able to give?

Reluctant to face him with pink, puffy lids, she bathed her eyes in cold water and, having applied make-up with care, decided she'd pass muster. But even then she lingered over her dressing until she had no possible excuse for further procrastination.

When she got to the kitchen, Saul, his movements economical and controlled, was making coffee. He was dressed in a dark well-cut business suit.

Glancing up, he said with cool courtesy, 'A little while ago I had a call from my agent. Some urgent business has cropped up which means that later on this morning I have to go to town. Can you be ready to come with me?'

It was phrased as a question but she guessed that in reality she had little choice. 'Well, I—' she began.

'Don't sound too eager.' The words had an edge.

She sighed. 'It's my *hair*. How can I go to London looking like Little Orphan Annie?'

Crisply, he told her, 'I've things to do in the village first, arrangements to make for our wedding, and you have a nine-thirty appointment at the hairdresser. We'll go straight on from there.'

Handing her a cup of coffee, he continued evenly, 'You'll need an overnight case. I intend to stay in town for a couple of days. It will give you an opportunity to choose a wedding-dress and shop for a trousseau... Mrs Hawkins will take care of Beth.'

Everything went smoothly and they were in London well before lunchtime. Autumn had presumed they would be staying at a hotel, but Saul drove to the underground car park of Morningdale Court, a modern apartment block not far from Piccadilly.

Having let them into the fifth-floor service flat, he gave her a spare key. 'You'd better have this, then you'll be free to come and go as you please.'

The small flat was nicely furnished but impersonal. 'It's really only a *pied-à-terre*,' he told her as he showed her round, 'but I wanted somewhere to stay when I had to be in town overnight.' Harshly, he added, 'I hated the thought of hotels.'

Being blind, he would have.

Not daring to make any comment, Autumn swallowed a lump in her throat and, peering into the tiny kitchen, got down to practicalities. 'Will I need to do any shopping?'

He shook his head. 'Not the kind you're thinking of. We'll eat out... And speaking of eating, having had nothing more than a slice of toast for breakfast, you must be ready for lunch?'

'I am, rather.'

'Come on, then... We've one stop to make first.'

They took a taxi to Bond Street, but only when they drew up outside an exclusive jeweller's shop did Autumn realise what Saul had in mind.

After a low-toned conversation between Saul and the grey-haired, dignified manager, she found herself staring at a tray of rings that took her breath away. They looked so quietly magnificent, that, afraid to choose, she glanced helplessly at Saul.

Without hesitation, he picked out an exquisite emerald in a simple gold setting. 'This one, I think.' When he slipped it on to her finger it was a perfect fit. 'Like it?'

Unable to speak, she nodded.

If he'd kissed her then, her joy would have been complete. But with a casual, 'Keep it on,' he turned away, pulling out his cheque-book.

Half an hour later they were being shown to a table in a fashionable restaurant close by. Glancing at the well-dressed women present, Autumn was thankful that her appearance at least wouldn't disgrace Saul.

She was wearing a dark brown Figuero suit she'd bought on Fifth Avenue, and after skilful cutting her hair now hugged her well-shaped head like a cap of smooth bronze feathers.

They were drinking their pre-lunch sherry when a tall, striking woman in the wake of a waiter suddenly stopped by their table. 'Well, if it isn't Saul!'

Rising to his feet, he inclined his head politely. 'Joanna.'

Never taking her eyes from his face, she said, 'Long time no see.'

'How very true,' Saul agreed smoothly, and Autumn knew the words had been carefully chosen.

Stunning as ever, Joanna was dressed in a gold turban and a flamboyant gold-mesh tunic with a matching miniskirt and thigh-length boots.

Looking at her, Autumn immediately felt old-fashioned and dowdy.

Without even a glance at the fair, slimly built young man hovering by her elbow, Joanna remarked, 'I see you have a table for four. May we join you?'

His dark face inscrutable, Saul answered, 'Please do.'

When the waiter, having seated them and provided additional menus, moved away, Joanna, her eyes still fixed on Saul, said briefly, 'This is David Gish—he's with the modelling agency. David, Saul Cresswell.'

Plainly thrown by the course of events, David Gish half rose and, reaching across the table to shake hands, muttered, 'How do you do?'

'How do you do?' Saul returned civilly. 'May I introduce you to Autumn Milski?'

When Autumn had smiled and shaken the extended hand, Saul turned to her and said casually, 'You remember Joanna, don't you, darling?'

Still reeling from the shock of Joanna's sudden appearance, Autumn replied with as much composure as she could muster, 'Yes, of course. How are you?'

Forced to acknowledge the younger woman's presence, Joanna ignored the civilities. 'I thought you were living in the States somewhere.'

'I was, but when my parents died I decided to come back to England.'

The news appeared to be anything but welcome. A coating of saccharine barely disguising the venom, Joanna purred, 'So Saul's taken little Autumn under his wing again.'

With a cool smile, Autumn demurred, 'Hardly little. I'm at least as tall as you are.'

'Perhaps I meant *young*.'

And insignificant was left unspoken but hung on the air.

'I'm twenty-two,' Autumn said, adding sweetly, 'Not particularly young, unless of course one's looking at it from the wrong side of thirty.'

Watching Joanna's carmine lips tighten, Autumn knew she'd held her own in that little skirmish.

Saul glanced her way, and, though his face was straight, she caught a gleam of surprised amusement in his grey eyes.

At that moment the waiter returned with a pad and pencil.

When the newcomers had ordered, Saul turned to Autumn, one dark brow raised interrogatively.

'I can't make up my mind what to have,' she said in honeyed tones. 'Won't you order for me, darling?' And she met his glinting look with a guileless face.

'I'm sure you'll enjoy the *soles aux crêpes*,' he said smoothly.

As the waiter moved away, Joanna returned her attention to Saul. 'I could hardly believe it when I heard you had your sight back.'

'How did you hear?'

'Quite by chance. I live in London now, so I'm not *au fait* with the Godsend gossip, but only a day or two ago I ran into an old school-friend of mine who was in town. She told me. I was so *pleased*.'

'How kind,' Saul murmured.

Ignoring the cool disdain in the words, she went on, 'I tried to get in touch with you, but that housekeeper of yours was no help—she just said you were away—and neither your agent nor your publisher seemed willing to tell me where you were...'

Sounding unconcerned, Saul asked, 'Why did you want to get in touch with me?'

She pouted at his tone. 'I thought it would be nice to see you, *chéri*, to have dinner together and talk over old times. After all, we were once very close.' And could be again, her intimate little smile suggested.

Autumn began to feel sick. She knew the technique of old. But surely Saul wouldn't be fool enough to fall for it a second time? Or would he? If he was still in love with Joanna…

His face showing only polite interest, he asked blandly, 'If we did meet to talk over old times, were you thinking of bringing your husband?'

Just for a second Joanna looked disconcerted, then, rallying, she said lightly, 'Oh, Carl and I have been divorced for almost six months now.'

'I hear the Carlton Danning finance company got into…difficulties, and he was made bankrupt?'

Her face suddenly hardening, Joanna said scathingly, 'He was always a fool.'

'But a rich one? At least, when you met him.'

She shrugged. 'On paper.'

Their food came, and while Joanna and Saul carried on talking, Autumn began to eat the fish and pancakes she no longer had any stomach for.

Since his muttered, 'How do you do?' David Gish had never once opened his mouth. Looking gloomy, ill at ease, he was obviously wishing himself anywhere but where he was.

Glancing up, she caught his eye and, feeling sorry for him, was about to engage him in conversation when he looked hastily away. Head down, concentrating on his meal, clearly all he wanted was for lunch to be over.

'Then you're *both* staying in town?' Joanna's voice was raised, sharp with jealous anger.

'For a couple of days.'

'At your flat?'

'Who told you I had a flat?'

'Your agent.'

'Ah, yes, Gerald…' Flicking back his cuff, Saul glanced at the thin gold Rolex that had replaced the Braille watch he'd been wearing. 'I ought to get moving. He and I have a meeting shortly.'

He signalled to the waiter and, waving away David Gish's awkward offer to split the bill, paid for the four of them. Then, turning to Autumn, who was about to rise, he said, 'No need to rush, darling—stay and have some coffee before you start your shopping spree. If you take a taxi to Knightsbridge, I've an account at Harrods which I've cleared for you to use. But in case you need some ready cash…' With a careless generosity that was like a blow in the face, he took a wad of notes from his wallet and dropped them into her lap, before touching his lips lightly to hers.

David Gish was already on his feet, waiting for Joanna, when, sharply dismissive, she said, 'I've a job lined up for this afternoon. I'll ring you later.'

His ears going red, his eyes fixed on no one in particular, he mumbled, 'Thanks for the lunch,' and bolted.

Slipping a possessive hand through Saul's arm, Joanna suggested, 'I'm going in your direction—perhaps we can share a taxi?'

'Why not?' he agreed lazily. Then, to Autumn, 'This evening Gerald's having a cocktail party for some film producer. Against my better judgement I've agreed to be there, so I doubt if I'll be back at the flat until after seven. If you get hungry before then, there's a restaurant on the ground floor. Have something sent up.'

Sitting with her head high, Autumn watched them walk away together and died a little.

Though she was wearing his ring, Saul hadn't introduced

her as his fiancée, nor had he mentioned their forthcoming marriage.

If it still was forthcoming.

It couldn't have taken him long to realise that, now he could see again, Joanna was more than willing to pick up where they'd left off, so perhaps he'd changed his plans and didn't intend to go through with the wedding?

But in that case why had he encouraged her to shop for a trousseau she wouldn't need?

Not that she had any intention of using his account, or spending a penny of the money he'd almost thrown at her...

Agitation threatening her veneer of calm, Autumn stuffed the wad of notes into her bag and rose to go, shaking her head at the coffee which was just arriving.

Outside it was dull and cold, a chilly wind flapping the gold and blue awning and chasing several discarded pamphlets along the gutter.

Instead of taking a taxi to Harrods, feeling only a kind of leaden emptiness, she walked the streets for hours, looking blindly in shop-windows filled with Christmas goods and glitter.

Even when dusk fell and it started to rain, the myriad lights gleaming on black roads and wet pavements, she kept walking. Finally, soaked to the skin and shivering, her ankle throbbing painfully, hardly knowing how she had got there, she found herself outside Morningdale Court.

A hot shower and a change of clothes brought life back into her limbs but did nothing to warm the cold misery inside.

Finding some tea-bags in the kitchen, she had just made and drunk a cup of milkless tea when the doorbell rang.

Wondering if it was one of the service staff, she opened the door.

Without waiting for an invitation, Joanna, dressed for the evening, walked straight in.

'Saul isn't back yet,' Autumn said flatly.

'I'm quite aware of that. I came to talk to you.'

The last thing she wanted was a tête-à-tête with Joanna but, making an effort to behave in a civilised manner, she asked, 'Would you like to sit down?'

The blonde shook her head. 'What I have to say won't take long.'

Her attention focused on Autumn's left hand, and she stared at the ring through narrowed eyes. 'When I noticed it at lunchtime I thought a stone that size must only be costume jewellery...' Spitefully, she added, 'I don't care for emeralds myself; they look like bits of coloured glass. I'd have chosen a diamond solitaire.'

Autumn took a deep breath. 'Did Saul tell you we're going to be married?'

'He told me he'd bought you a ring. However, I don't think you'll be keeping it long.' Viciously, Joanna added, 'You must have thought you were very clever to hook him finally, but you've lost out, sweetie. I'm back in his life, and apparently just in the nick of time.'

Through a tight throat, Autumn said, 'You've walked out on him once. What makes you think he wants you back?'

'He's always been mad about me, and I feel the same way about him. I was a fool to leave him. But how did I know he was going to regain his sight...?'

'If you didn't want him when he was blind you can't really love him.'

'And you do?'

'Yes.'

Joanna's beautiful lips twisted. 'Well, don't try to tell me *he* loves *you*. I know perfectly well why he wants to marry you. He was hurt and angry when I married someone else, and he's determined to get back at me... But it won't take me long to soften him up… So I'm warning you, don't try and hold on to him. It won't work. Tell him you've changed your mind, before he tells you. At least it will salvage a bit of your pride.' She turned to the door.

Autumn lifted her chin. 'When he gets back—'

'I doubt very much if he'll *be* back tonight.' The blonde fired her parting shot triumphantly. 'After he leaves that cocktail party he's having dinner with me…at my place.'

Watching the door close behind the model's tall, slender figure, Autumn knew with dreadful certainty that Joanna had been right about why Saul had decided to marry her.

It explained everything, fitted far too well not to be the truth. He had wanted to get his own back, not only on her, but on Joanna as well.

Now, knowing Joanna was free again, he was almost certainly regretting it, and when he eventually got home he would no doubt make it clear that the wedding was off.

But she couldn't bear to wait around just to have him confirm that, for the second time, Joanna had won. Better to go now.

Icy cold, filled with a terrible numbing ache of despair, Autumn bundled her few belongings back into the case, and seized her bag and mac.

Unfastening the opal, which she'd worn since the night Saul had returned it to her, she left that, her ring, the money he'd given her and the key to the flat on the coffee-table, and shut the door behind her.

Head down, she was stepping from the lift into the foyer, when she found her way blocked by a tall, broad-shouldered figure.

'Running out on me?' Saul enquired silkily.

Her heart thudding against her ribs, she said foolishly, 'I wasn't expecting you.'

'Obviously not.' His face was so bleak and set that it

frightened her. Taking the case from her nerveless fingers, he gripped her upper arm and hustled her back into the lift.

'I could have saved you the trouble of packing if I'd come up at once, but I arrived to find Joanna just leaving, and paused to put her straight on a few things.'

Once in the flat he tossed aside the case and, having shed his tie and jacket, propelled Autumn into the bedroom, closing the door. 'Now it's time *you* got something straight. You still owe me.'

His back to the panels, he discarded his shoes and socks and began to unbutton his shirt, ordering with a kind of raging calm, 'Take off your clothes.'

'Wh-what?' she stammered.

'Get your clothes off before I'm tempted to tear them off. I'm going to collect on the debt.' His shirt and trousers were sloughed, to be swiftly followed by his silk briefs.

Catching her breath, she cried, 'No...I won't let you use and humiliate me any more. If you touch me, I'll scream.'

'Scream away,' he invited, advancing on her.

Unwilling, as well he'd known, to cause a disturbance, she resisted silently but furiously while, ruthlessly, he stripped her.

Even when she was naked she continued to struggle, fighting tooth and nail, until, muttering, 'You little hell-cat,' he threw her on to the bed and used his weight to pin her there.

One flailing fist caught him hard on the cheekbone, and at his sharp exclamation, suddenly terrified she might have endangered his sight, she froze.

Gripping her wrists, he pressed her hands into the pillows, one on each side of her head, and, breathing hard, stared down at her.

Her eyes tightly closed, she whispered, 'Saul...are you all right?'

'Am *I* all right?' He sounded startled.

'Your eyes...'

Suddenly comprehending, he said huskily, 'Oh, Autumn...' Then, 'Yes, quite all right.'

Relief brought tears that forced themselves beneath her closed lids and ran down her cheeks.

'Don't cry,' he said almost fiercely, but, once started, unable to stop the flood of built-up tension and emotion from pouring out, she began to sob.

Rolling over, he gathered her shaking body into his arms and pulled the bedclothes over them.

She cried until she had no tears left, then lay against him, spent and hiccuping.

After a while, when the hiccups had stopped, he asked quietly, 'Why were you leaving me?'

She sniffed dismally. 'I realised Joanna was right...'

'When she said what?'

'That you were marrying me just to get your own back on her.'

'She was wrong. What else did she say?'

'That after the cocktail party you were going to her place for dinner.'

'It shows how little she knows me.'

'Then you weren't...?'

'She asked me to go. She seemed to think she only had to lift her little finger to get me back.'

'Even though she ran out on you when you needed her most?'

'So did you.' The quietly spoken words shook her.

Pushing herself up on one elbow, Autumn looked at him. 'But you—you *told* me to run,' she protested helplessly.

He sat up too, his face hardening. 'And you did, like a frightened rabbit, all the way to America.'

'You told me to get out of your life and stay out. You said, "If I ever set eyes on you again we might both be sorry"...'

With a short, sharp sigh, he admitted, 'I was furiously angry then... But later, when I wanted you, though you'd sworn you loved me, you wouldn't come.' He laughed harshly. 'It's funny really—neither of the women who pretended to love me could bear to love a blind man. Though, I have to say, Joanna tried harder than you did.'

Blankly, Autumn said, 'I don't understand what you mean...'

'You understand perfectly well. As soon as I was able to have visitors, I asked for you. But you never came... And when I finally got out of hospital, I heard you'd left for the States...'

'You asked for me?' Her voice was barely above a whisper.

'Oh, come on, Autumn,' he said wearily. 'What's the use of pretending you didn't know?'

'But I didn't know...' Then, sharply, 'And I don't believe it. You were the one who refused to see me.'

'Don't give me that,' he said harshly. 'It was my eyesight I lost, not my reason.'

'But that's what the ward sister told me.'

'Don't lie to me, Autumn. I know quite well you never came within a mile of the hospital. That's the thing I can't forgive...'

'But I—'

'You admitted you didn't shed a single tear when you heard I was blind, so why lie about this?'

'I'm not lying.' When he would have interrupted, she put her hand to his lips. 'Please, Saul, *listen* to me.'

'Very well.' Narrowed eyes on her face, he waited.

She spoke quietly, but with passionate truth. 'As soon as I heard about the accident from Joanna I went straight to the Royal Infirmary, but the doctor wouldn't let me see you...'

Saul's expression was still sceptical. Knowing she had

to convince him, she went on, 'You were on the third floor of the East Wing, in the intensive care unit… For the next seventy-two hours I never left the hospital. All the nurses were very nice to me, but one of the staff nurses was particularly kind. She was plump and dark-haired and spoke with a Scottish accent. Her name was Ruth.

'She arranged for me to have a folding bed in one of the empty cubicles and told me I could eat in the staff canteen and borrow the visitors' bathroom. She even loaned me some clean undies.

'When you came out of Intensive Care you were transferred to a room that was part of Harry Duncton Ward. At least, that was the official name, but the nurses all called it Harry's.

'I asked to be allowed to see you. The ward sister refused.' With a little mirthless smile, Autumn went on, 'She was called Sister Mercy, but she didn't live up to her name. When I begged, she just gave me a disapproving look and said you didn't want me there. Then I asked how you were and she told me you'd lost your sight…

'I didn't cry. Some grief is too deep for tears. I just stood there and wanted to die…'

Though his hand, lying on the counterpane, clenched involuntarily, Saul made no attempt to touch her.

'Later that afternoon, I tried again to see you. I—I thought you might be alone, but Sister Mercy said, "I can only suggest you go home; you look like a ghost. And, for your information, Mr Cresswell isn't alone. His fiancée is by his side"…'

'Oh, she was,' Saul agreed grimly, 'and she made sure she stayed by my side until she'd got rid of you.'

'You mean…?'

'I mean she played a very clever game. I wasn't the one who asked for you to be kept out. Just the opposite, in fact.

I *wanted* to talk to you, to tell you how sorry I was for what I'd done to you, to tell you…oh, all kinds of things…

'Joanna swore that she'd been to see you, and you wouldn't come anywhere near the hospital… I see now that it was pure malice on her part.'

Softly, lethally, he added, 'It's a good thing I didn't know this when I spoke to her a little while ago. I might have been tempted to break her beautiful neck. Most of my pain and anger, my need for revenge, was because I thought you'd run out on me…'

For a moment Autumn was filled with a fierce rage against the woman who had caused them both so much suffering. Then it died, leaving only a kind of weary calm. 'If she was so determined to have you herself, I don't understand why she ever left you.'

'To be fair to Joanna, one of the reasons was that she almost certainly realised I was obsessed by you… After I came out of hospital, our relationship never got back on the same footing. When I thought about making love to her, your face always came between us.'

Horrified, Autumn exclaimed, 'All because of my stupidity that night…'

'Oh, no.' He shook his head. 'Although I tried not to admit it even to myself, I'd wanted you since you were about fifteen, and the strength of that desire frightened me to death. It seemed almost indecent. I was nearly ten years older and a trusted friend.

'You were so damned young and innocent, with your wide-eyed hero-worship. I could imagine how horrified you'd be if you realised my true feelings, so I did my best to bury them.

'Then I met Joanna. Despite her faults she's quite a woman, and I transferred all my sexual frustration to her until the night of your eighteenth birthday.

'After that, nothing was the same again, and with a growing bitterness I almost came to blame you for every-thing…even for Joanna leaving me… Though with hind-sight I realise I should be grateful that she did.'

Still needing a final reassurance, needing to hear him put it into words, Autumn asked, 'So you don't intend to go back to her?'

'No, I do not.' A shade bitterly, he added, 'You are the only woman who's ever had me on a string. The only woman I want.'

She sighed, relief running through her like a glad tide. 'Then our wedding is still on?'

'No.' He spoke harshly. 'As from now you're free to go, so there's no need to sigh.'

'Oh, but I—'

'If you ever did owe me anything it's been paid in full. There are plenty of men who—'

Though he'd never said he loved her, he had said he wanted her. That was enough. It had to be. Prepared to fight now, she broke in with crisp finality, 'I'm through with men.'

'Don't be foolish, Autumn. You said yourself you want a home and family. Now you're no longer afraid of being frigid, you should find yourself a man you can really love.'

'I've found a man I can really love. A man I've loved since I was thirteen…' Ignoring the sudden blaze of hope that illuminated his dark face, she ploughed on, 'And where has it got me? All he'll admit to is an obsession, and he's so thick that—'

She stopped with a squeak as Saul grabbed hold of her and, pulling her across his lap, demanded threateningly, 'Who are you calling thick?'

Her arms slid round his neck and, her face pressed to the tanned column of his throat, she whispered, 'The man who wouldn't recognise real love if it came up and bit him in the neck.'

'God knows I *want* to believe you love me,' he said huskily. 'But after all I've put you through...'

After a moment, his cheek against her short, feathery hair, he went on, 'When you plumped for a church wedding, it gave me hope. Then, last night, when you came to me, I waited for you to say you loved me, but you didn't. You gave me everything except the one thing I really wanted.'

'I gave you that, only you didn't know it.'

'That night at Farthing Beck, when I asked indirectly if you still loved me, you shook your head.'

'How could I admit to loving you when I thought all you wanted was revenge?'

'I've been the worst kind of fool. Caused you a lot of pain.'

'That's over and done with. The only thing that does still grieve me is that all those years when you were blind and alone I could have been with you...'

'Perhaps it's better that you weren't. Even though I bought Cecilia Cottage to try to feel close to you, for a long time I was so bitter at losing my sight that I might have killed your love...'

As she began to shake her head, he said, 'I believe I needed those years alone to sort myself out... I've always felt very strongly that, ''To every thing there is a season, and a time to every purpose under the heaven''...and now—'

'It's high time you made an honest woman of me.' She hid her emotion beneath flippancy.

He laughed. 'How right you are, my love...'

Greatly daring, she asked, '*Do* you love me?'

'Haven't I told you?'

She shook her head. '''Want'' was the only four-letter word you used.'

Cradling her against him, he said, 'Well, if what I feel for you isn't love, it's a dead ringer for it.'

Her heart overflowing with joy, she informed him blithely, 'I'll settle for that, and an end to all our problems.'

Thoughtfully, he murmured, 'I still have a problem.'

Secure in his love, she asked serenely, 'What's that?'

'I'm going to have to rewrite my book…make it a happy ending. And I shall have to think of a new title. *The Tamarind Tree* is no longer appropriate: the tamarind has bitter fruit.'

'Then call it *The Singing Tree*,' she suggested. 'In the legend, anyone who finds the singing tree finds true happiness.' A little shyly, she added, 'The kind we're going to share when we're married.'

Having kissed her until she was dizzy with pleasure, he asked, 'Does that mean you want to wait until we're man and wife before we make love again?'

She pretended to consider, then remarked mischievously, 'I've always been told there's an added excitement to stolen fruit, and as it's one of my few remaining chances to go to bed with a man I'm not married to…'

'I'd better make sure you enjoy it… Before or after dinner?'

'Both,' she replied promptly.

When he'd finished laughing, he said, 'Darling Autumn,' and began to kiss her again.

It's romantic comedy with a kick
(in a pair of strappy pink heels)!

Introducing

"It's chick-lit with the romance and happily-ever-after ending that Harlequin is known for."
—*USA TODAY* bestselling author Millie Criswell, author of *Staying Single*, October 2003

"Even though our heroine may take a few false steps while finding her way, she does it with wit and humor."
—Dorien Kelly, author of *Do-Over*, November 2003

Launching October 2003.
Make sure you pick one up!

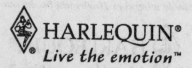

HARLEQUIN®
Live the emotion™

Visit us at www.harlequinflipside.com

The world's bestselling romance series.

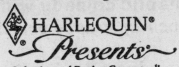

HARLEQUIN®
Presents

Seduction and Passion Guaranteed!

In 2003, we have fabulous new miniseries by all your favorite authors....

Which one are you waiting for?

Jane Porter's
THE GALVÁN BRIDES
In Dante's Debt
On sale January, #2298

Sandra Marton's
THE O'CONNELLS
Keir O'Connell's Mistress
On sale March, #2309

Penny Jordan's
ARABIAN NIGHTS
The Sheikh's Virgin Bride
On sale June, #2325

Miranda Lee's
THREE RICH MEN
A Rich Man's Revenge
On sale October, #2349

Jane Porter's
BRIDES OF L'AMOUR
The Frenchman's Love-Child
On sale November, #2355

Pick up a Harlequin Presents® novel and you will enter a world of spine-tingling passion and provocative, tantalizing romance!

Available wherever Harlequin books are sold.

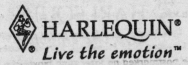

HARLEQUIN®
Live the emotion™

Visit us at www.eHarlequin.com

HPGEN03

Witchcraft, deceit and more...
all FREE from

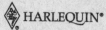

The world's bestselling romance series.

HARLEQUIN®
Presents

Seduction and Passion Guaranteed!

INTERNATIONAL
DOCTORS

They're guaranteed to raise your pulse!

**Meet the most eligible medical men of the world,
in a new series of stories, by popular authors,
that will make your heart race!**

**Whether they're saving lives or dealing with desire,
our doctors have got bedside manners that
send temperatures soaring....**

Coming in Harlequin Presents in 2003:

THE DOCTOR'S SECRET CHILD by Catherine Spencer
#2311, on sale March

THE PASSION TREATMENT by Kim Lawrence
#2330, on sale June

THE DOCTOR'S RUNAWAY BRIDE by Sarah Morgan
#2366, on sale December

**Pick up a Harlequin Presents® novel and you will enter a world
of spine-tingling passion and provocative, tantalizing romance!**

Available wherever Harlequin books are sold.

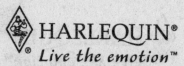

HARLEQUIN®
Live the emotion™

Visit us at www.eHarlequin.com

HPINTDOC

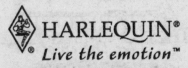

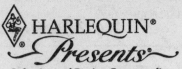

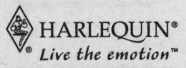